What others are saying about *The Missing Piece...*

"Mr. Boughton's book suggests it is written by an 'ordinary' guy writing for ordinary people. However, in the process he manages to expose something extraordinary-the reader's soul. If you are interested in marriage, divorce, parenting, business, faith, personal finance, or just lessons in living, Mr. Boughton's book provides that and more. His style will cause you to methodically explore the quality of your life, your relationships, and your existence. It will be a challenge to those reading his book to attempt to avoid inserting many of his thoughts into your next conversation, whether it be at home, at the office or socially. Mr. Boughton states that he wishes '...to give people the hope that tomorrow can always be better than today.' He succeeds."

> — *K. Mark Loyd, Judge*
> *Johnson County Circuit Court*
> *Franklin, Indiana*

"As Bud Boughton writes, his book is an effort by '...a middle-aged guy trying to make it in this world.' You certainly don't have to be middle-aged (or a guy) to benefit from this book, which provides valuable insights for readers of both genders and all ages. Bud provides a useful framework for dealing with life's events that readers of any age will be able to relate to their own lives. In particular, readers of the 'baby boomer' generation will find themselves reading this insightful book with a knowing smile; Bud Boughton's story is their story. Bud's experiences aren't of the shipwreck-survival-harrowing-rescue-from-Everest variety. Rather, they are experiences most of us face as human beings: illness; death; loss; divorce and the challenges of intergenerational relationships. Bud relates his process of growth and the insights that he's developed in a fashion that will help readers make sense of their own networks of relationships and experiences."

> — *Charles D. Frame, Ph.D., Managing Director*
> *Center for Healthcare Leadership*
> *Emory University School of Medicine*
> *Atlanta, Georgia*

"*The Missing Piece* is fresh, insightful and thought-provoking. And, best of all, it makes perfect sense. This book just might be 'The Missing Piece' that will make your life more productive and satisfying. Boughton's insights have timeless and universal truths that are even more meaningful and relevant since 9/11."

> — *The Rev. Joe Beavon, Th.D.*
> *Retired United Methodist Minister and*
> *Non-Profit Fundraiser*
> *Old Hickory, TN*

"Yes, life is puzzling for most of us. And we may never 'find' all the pieces that make it work or fit together. Boughton lets us get a grasp into combining a clearer picture of ourselves and those around us who help us complete the task of our inner puzzles."

> — *Harris Warsaw, Vice President,*
> *General Business, North America*
> *IBM, Inc.*

"In today's unsettled world, more than ever before, people are looking for answers on how to find that 'missing piece.' Bud's open and heartfelt journey through the challenges he has faced provide both inspiration and a compass to help us face life's many challenges. I found his sensitive, provocative and sincere discussion of life's diverse challenges both thought provoking and directional..."

> — *Randy E. DeMont*
> *Executive Vice President & General Manager*
> *Worldwide Sales, Service & Support*
> *Hitachi Data Systems, Denver, CO*

"A very thought-provoking, motivational book that makes you stop and reprioritize your life and challenges you to focus on what's really important."

> — *Ken LaRose, Client Liaison/Community*
> *Engagement Specialist*
> *Fanning Howey Associates*
> *Carmel, Indiana*

The Missing Piece

Our Search for Security in an Insecure World

Harold "Bud" Boughton

Second Edition
Originally published in 2003.

Originally published by Lucky Press, LLC

Author's Website: www.budboughton.com
Front cover design by Bart Leonard, www.bart-leonard.com
Book design by Janice Phelps Williams   .

To contact the author or for special sales to organizations, please e-mail coachb@budboughton.com.

Library of Congress Cataloging-in-Publication Data

Boughton, Harold "Bud".
   The missing piece : our search for security in an insecure world / Harold "Bud" Boughton.
   p. cm.
   ISBN   978-0-9846317-8-0 (alk. paper)
   1. Security (Psychology) I. Title.

BF575.S35 B68   2002
   155.9--dc21   2002004544

❧

Dedication

This book is dedicated to all of the innocent people who lost their lives in the terrorist attacks of September 11, 2001.

This includes all those who were killed in the World Trade Center towers in New York City, members of the New York City Fire Department, the New York City Police Department and other emergency rescue workers killed while responding to the emergency, those killed at the Pentagon, and those on American Airlines flight 11, United Airlines flight 175, American Airlines flight 77 and United Airlines flight 93.

Each of these people was a "piece" in someone else's puzzle. Now, we remember them and honor them knowing that they will always be a piece of an even bigger puzzle, the world's puzzle.

God bless each and every one of them.

Table of Contents

Acknowledgments

Had I known how much time and effort would be involved when I began writing this book, I am not sure I would have embarked on the project in the first place. As is anything in life, we don't accomplish much on our own. In reality, our individual accomplishments are collective efforts because of our connections to other people. Such is the case with this book.

First I want to thank Lori Siragusa, a dear friend, a tough critic, a positive influence and yes, the individual who consistently inspired me to persevere and ultimately complete this book. Thank you, Lori, for all of your help, support and friendship as I wrote this book and over the past fifteen years. I also want to thank a brilliant, young, creative artist, Bart Leonard, who is currently a student at Franklin College. Coaching college football for the last few seasons at Franklin College with Bart's dad (Head Coach Mike Leonard), I got to know Bart and became aware of his talents as an artist. So, I decided to have Bart take a shot at designing the cover for this, the 2nd Edition of *The Missing Piece* and I couldn't have been more pleased with the outcome. Thank you, Bart, for designing a thought-provoking and memorable cover. Also, I must thank Janice Phelps Williams and her sister, Joan, both of whom were with Lucky Press LLC when I first presented my manuscript to them back in 2000. When so many others said "No," without even taking time to review my manuscript, you chose to take the time and in the end, said, "Yes!" I don't know if I would have ever gotten the book published if it were not for you both. So, my sincere thanks to you both.

Along the way, I have been blessed to have many special "pieces" in my puzzle. My parents, Anne and Bud Boughton, my two brothers, John and Rick; my two sons, Brad and Cory and their mother, Jackie (my first wife), and so many dear friends — they are all part of who I am today. Their presence in my life helped make this book a reality. But, most of all, I must acknowledge and thank Cindy, my loving wife, for her never-ending patience with me and her willingness to allow me to work long hours on this project when we could have been doing so many other things together. Cindy, you are an angel, a true blessing in my life and a very, very special piece in my puzzle.

A Special Note

I think it is important for you to know that this book was written, for the most part, from August 2000 to May 2001. In fact, I was getting ready to submit my finished manuscript to several publishing houses for review when our world was turned totally upside down by the events of September 11, 2001. While the theme of my book was always going to be about how we all seek to find some sense of security in our lives, never in my wildest dreams or worst nightmares did I ever imagine the horrific carnage that would occur on September 11, 2001 — carnage that would change our lives as Americans forever.

Following the events of September 11, I thought about maybe going back and rewriting the entire book. I felt that maybe I needed to rethink the content of each chapter and ultimately, the lessons I have learned in my own life, which I share in the final three chapters. I thought I might need to do this since I had written this book based largely on my personal experiences and that maybe I would need to incorporate more information related to what has been a life-changing tragedy for each and every one of us Americans.

While I did take the time to go back and reread the entire book, do additional editing and make some minor additions; for the most part, I chose not to rewrite the book. Here is the reason why.

When I wrote this book, I wrote it because I wanted to give people hope that tomorrow can always be better than today. That no matter what our circumstances, our fears or sorrows, no matter how perplexed we find ourselves or how much anxiety we are dealing with, we can always hope and believe in our hearts that tomorrow may be just a little bit better. It is because of that purpose, that intention, that I decided not to rewrite the book as a result of September 11, (other than the dedication to those who lost their lives and this special note).

Like all Americans, I have been confused and angered by the horrific events of that dark September day. How much hate can someone have in his or her heart to commit such an act? What was their motive? What were they really trying to prove?

One thing is certain, our perception of life in America, our reality, changed that day. It forced us to realize that we are not immune from the ugliness and ills that we previously believed only existed elsewhere. We live on the same planet; we are all part of the same world. However, as I write this special note some sixty-five days after what was certainly one of the darkest days in American history, one thing has already been made very clear to me. As a country, we may be more united than ever before.

And one other thing is very clear — yes, there is hope for a better tomorrow.

—Harold "Bud" Boughton, November 15, 2001

Preface

I actually started to write this book back in 1990, some twenty-one years ago. I was thirty-nine years old at the time and I had always had this ambition, this secret desire, to write a book. I just had one small problem that was holding me back. I had no idea what to write about.

That all changed on a Sunday in September of 1990 while I was sitting in Chicago O'Hare International Airport waiting to board a flight. Don't ask me "how" or "why" but all of a sudden, out of the blue, it hit me, and some 12 years later (2002), *The Missing Piece: Our Search for Security in an Insecure World* was a reality.

The inspiration for this book actually came as a result of a painful divorce I went through in 1989. Married for sixteen years, my wife told me she wanted a divorce. At the time, our two sons were just thirteen and nine years old. I was devastated (lost seventeen pounds in thirty days) and really, did not know how I was ever going to survive the ordeal. In less than four months, I went from being a happily married, thirty-nine-year-old, upper middle class guy with two wonderful sons to an unhappily divorced, financially struggling, middle class guy who had lost his family, his house, and subsequently, would lose his job. In other words, I was just an ordinary, everyday kind of guy who thought everything was right in my life when suddenly my world came crashing down around me.

As I lived through this rather painful period in my life, I started to look at the world and myself more closely and wondered why the world I had come from was so different from the one I was now living in. The differences were startling.

When I grew up in the late fifties and early sixties in a place called Kenmore, New York, (suburb of Buffalo) divorce was almost unheard of. In fact, I did not have a single close friend whose parents had gone through a divorce. But in 1989, divorce was hardly uncommon and like it or not, I was forced to deal with this reality.

When I was growing up, nobody had ever heard the terms "downsizing" and "right-sizing" and men in gray flannel suits worked for the same company for twenty-five or thirty years. I know this; my dad was one of those men. But in the late eighties and early nineties, mergers and acquisitions became daily occurrences and no one's job was safe in the workplace. I learned this lesson less than six months after my divorce was finalized when I was "fired" from the software company I worked for. This, too, was a devastating experience.

Even simple things like family dinners had seemed to disappear from this world I was now living in. When I was a kid, families used to sit down and eat dinner together every night, discussing the events of the day. In 1990, however, I would often see kids eating McDonald's cheeseburgers and fries in the back seat of the car as Mom drove home, all the while conducting business on her cell phone. And that was...dinner?

Certainly, I was struggling with my own personal situation, but even more so, I was struggling with everything I saw going on around me. The world I had grown up in was no longer the world I knew. Where were the values and the sense of commitment that I experienced when I was being brought up? Is this really what our lives have come to? I continued to ask myself the same question, "Where in this world is there any security?" The irony of it all was the fact that if there was one thing at that point in my life that I thought was really solid, really secure, it was my marriage. How wrong I was.

So, that Sunday in O'Hare Airport, I decided to write a book on this subject and in 2002, *The Missing Piece* was published. It is important to note that this book would have never become a reality had it not been for my very supportive wife, a wonderful publisher who believed in me, and a marketing professional who prodded me along. Because of them, I became a published author. Now, some nine years later after its original release, Lucky Press LLC and I have agreed to work together and release what is a second edition of *The Missing Piece*.

The book's content will be almost identical to the first edition, but I did choose to re-write this, the Preface. After all, a lot has changed in my life since this book was originally published in 2002.

I'm older now (sixty) and my sons are now in their thirties. Brad, my older son, is married and he and his wife now have a beautiful little girl (Lilianne) making me officially a grandfather. I am still married to Cindy, my childhood sweetheart from my elementary school days (a second marriage for us both); and we now have six grandchildren between us, five of which have come into this world in the last nine years. As our extended family grows on both sides, I realize even more how blessed I am to have Cindy in my life as my wife and best friend.

Professionally speaking, my last nine years have been a bit of a roller coaster ride. I've had some really great years (with great earnings) and some absolutely horrible years. Some of my biggest setbacks and disappointments professionally involved colleagues who I trusted and who I thought believed in me. Unfortunately,

I learned the hard way that even when performing at a very high level number-wise, anyone can become a disposable item in the corporate world. Call it bad timing, bad karma, whatever — but when the cards are dealt, you have to live with them. The economy hasn't helped matters either, once again raising issues related to our security. And yet, out of bad always comes some good. The disappointment and ugliness in my professional life led me back to an opportunity to coach college football again, something I have enjoyed to no end! In fact, becoming a college football coach was my career ambition when I was attending college some forty years ago! Couple this with the opportunity to write a second book which was published in 2005 (*Dad's Last Letter: Leadership Principles for the Next Generation*), and I realize that in the big picture of life, I have continued to be blessed countless times over in the past nine years. Yes, life is good!

In preparing to re-release *The Missing Piece*, I sat down and re-read the entire book, cover-to-cover. As I read it, it took me back in time but it also made me realize something. I realized that I still feel very much the same about the message(s) in the book. In fact, if anything, my experiences over the last nine years have intensified my feelings and my passion for the content of *The Missing Piece*; especially the content of the final four chapters.

While the world has continued to evolve and change over the past nine years and while some of these changes have impacted me financially, emotionally, physically and spiritually — despite all of the changes, the ups and downs, and disappointments, I am still pretty much the same person. My vision for hope is unchanged and despite some negative times professionally, I still believe that tomorrow will always hold the promise and the possibility of being just a little bit better than today! Nothing has changed my demeanor or attitude when it comes to that way of thinking.

Preface

I knew when I began to write this book (1990) that the writing process would be a bit of a therapeutic exercise, forcing me to ask questions of myself and confront some of my insecurities in the process. Interestingly, re-reading the book some nine years after its original release took on the form of its own therapeutic exercise. As I read the book now, I find myself asking a lot of the same questions but the insecurities and concerns that I now face are totally different from those in my past. Ah, the mystery of life!

For you, the reader, please know that when I originally wrote this book, my purpose and hope was that it might provide insightful thoughts, new and different perspectives, and help you, the reader, to become more introspective about your own life. I guess you could say I wanted to help people find their other missing peace. Nine years later, all I can say is that my heart is still in the same place and maybe that's what matters most of all.

I hope you enjoy the book and that someday you do find your missing peace.

See you at Mirror Lake.

PART I

Introduction
"The Missing Piece"

This was terrible. The absolute worst! Billy pressed his nose against the window and felt the cold dampness of the October rain. It was Saturday morning. The leaves were peaking, the colors absolutely brilliant, spilling hues of gold, red and orange across the mountainside. As he looked out of his grandfather's log cabin cottage, he was a very disappointed little boy. Yes, it was raining all right — no, make that pouring — and for a ten-year-old who had looked forward, for months, to spending this weekend with his grandfather at Mirror Lake, nothing could be worse.

Billy's parents had planned way back in June to attend a business conference in New York City on this weekend. Ever since, Billy had been looking forward to the weekend with his "Papa," the name he affectionately called his grandfather. He and Papa were going to hike through the woods, go fishing, build a campfire outside in the evenings and even climb up Whiteface Mountain together. It was going to be the best weekend Billy and Papa had ever spent together! And now, all those plans were down the drain.

Billy turned away from the window and looked at the cozy interior of the small, five-room cottage. This place, Papa's cottage, was a very special, almost magical, kind of place to Billy. It was located in Lake Placid, New York, on a beautiful little lake called Mirror Lake, nestled in the heart of the Adirondack Mountains. Billy cherished his visits to the cottage because Papa always had a way of making those times interesting and so much fun. Every time Billy visited Papa's cottage, he seemed to learn something new and felt like he came away more grown up than when he had arrived. Billy always thought the cottage was a perfect place, warm and cozy in the winter months and yet the darkness of the interior kept it cool and comfortable on hot summer days. It had a rustic look to it, something that gave it character. And on this morning, with a fire crackling in the stone fireplace and the fragrance of Papa's special blueberry pancakes coming from the kitchen, even with the lousy weather, it was perfect. Even though he was only ten years old, Billy knew this was a special place, his special place.

But, it was pouring rain outside. What were they going to do with their day?

Suddenly a voice boomed from the kitchen, "All right Billy, get in here for some of Papa's world famous blueberry pancakes. We've got a big day ahead of us." Billy ran to the kitchen where he feasted his eyes on a stack of three blueberry pancakes.

The kitchen was equally as cozy as the living area of the cottage. Old white appliances of 1960 vintage, a double sink with worn porcelain rested beneath the kitchen window, simple, oak kitchen cabinets and a round, oak table with just two chairs. The hardwood floors were shiny in the corners but worn in front of the stove and sink. A braided rug, a Christmas gift from Billy's mom and dad, covered most of the kitchen floor. No dishwasher in Papa's house, just a strainer by the sink where dishes lived. They never seemed to make it back into the cupboards where they belonged. No microwave oven either, which was a source of mild family controversy. Billy's mom said that not having a microwave oven in these times was a classic example of Papa's stubborn nature. Billy's mom and dad had even given Papa a small microwave for his birthday just two years ago and were not very happy when they learned he had given it as "a gift" to the concession stand down by the lake where Billy and Papa went ice skating in the winter. Papa had said a lot more people would benefit from the microwave this way, but everyone in Billy's family knew the real reason he gave it away was because of his firm belief and conviction that everyone in this world was in too much of a hurry.

Billy liked this quality in his grandfather. Billy's mom and dad were always in a hurry and never seemed to have time to do fun things. Papa, on the other hand, was never in too much of a hurry to spend time with Billy. Come to think of it, Papa was never in too much of a hurry to do anything. He seemed to take his time at almost everything he did, living and savoring every moment of every experience.

Billy finished his last bite of pancakes and carried his dishes to the sink to rinse them off. "Papa, what are we going to do today? This weather stinks! It's ruined all of our plans."

"William, William," Papa responded. Billy did not like being addressed by his real name, William. However, when Papa called him by this name, it was different. When Papa said Billy's formal name, William, he always said it twice and with a booming voice. Billy knew that this was just one other way that his grandfather liked to have fun with him, but it made Billy feel important and the absolute center of attention.

"William, William, my good man, you fret about the wrong things. Our plans have not been ruined, they have merely been changed. I believe that when the sun sets tonight, this will have been one of the best days we have ever spent together." Papa spoke the words with such boldness, even if mocking himself a little. They rolled off his lips with authority and he pointed his finger in the air as he finished his bold prediction.

Billy giggled with excitement, almost forgetting the torrential downpour outside. Papa had a plan and whatever it was, Billy was filled with curiosity and anticipation just thinking about what they might end up doing with their day. Papa always had something special in mind and he never seemed to let anything spoil his ability to have fun and make the best of any situation. That was one of the things that made Papa such a very special person to Billy. But, what could it be that Papa had in mind that would make this rainy Saturday so special?

Papa disappeared from the kitchen into his bedroom. Billy could see the glow from Papa's closet light in the bedroom and while his curiosity was aroused, he stayed in the kitchen. He heard Papa shuffling through things in the closet. What could Papa be up to?

"Eureka! My boy, I've found it!"

Billy wondered what could it be that deserved such a loud and rousing proclamation from his grandfather. Papa entered the kitchen with a dust-covered box about the size of a shoebox, only a little flatter and wider.

"Follow me," Papa said as he made his way from the kitchen back into the larger living area of the cottage. Billy was right behind him.

Papa sat down on the large leather couch and began clearing everything off the large rectangular coffee table that sat in front of the fireplace. The rain was pouring on the roof but the fireplace warmed the room and Billy was filled with excitement. This was going to be a great day after all. But what did Papa have in the box?

The table was cleared. Papa adopted a very serious countenance, but Billy knew this was how Papa liked to have fun with him. "Billy, we have a challenge ahead of us and if we are the honorable men I believe we are, we will overcome this challenge." Papa winked at Billy. He picked up the box, blew the dust off the top of it toward the center of the room and then, gingerly and oh so carefully, removed the top of the box as though it were filled with valuable gems made of diamonds and gold. Papa then poured hundreds of pieces of a jigsaw puzzle onto the coffee table.

"Cool!" Billy shrieked with delight, "We're going to make this puzzle today!"

"That's correct," answered Papa, "but only if we're up to the challenge. This puzzle has five hundred pieces and it won't be an easy one."

"What will it look like when it's done, Papa? What's it a picture of?"

Papa wiped the remaining dust off the top of the box with the sleeve of his black-and-red-checkered flannel shirt and handed the top to Billy. Billy looked at what was to him one of the most beautiful pictures he had ever seen. It was a majestic, snow-covered mountain peak rising high above a forest of evergreens and hardwood plants, with a beautiful lake in the foreground. The beautiful blue sky and the sun shining brightly on the scene, clearly made for what was surely a picture post card print being sold in souvenir and gift shops to tourists somewhere.

"This is beautiful, Papa. Where is this place? Where is this mountain? Can we go climb it when we're done making the puzzle and..." The questions were coming faster than Papa could answer them, and the old man began to laugh at the boy's eagerness and excitement.

"William, William," Papa declared as he laughed loudly before trailing off into a wheezing cough, "it is indeed a beautiful place, isn't it?" Papa paused for just a minute to catch his breath.

"Let me tell you about this place, Billy. This mountain is known as Mount Rainier, and it is located in the state of Washington way out on the Western Coast of the United States."

"I know where that is, Papa. I've seen the state of Washington on a map of the United States." Billy liked to try to impress his Papa with how smart he was even though he was only ten years old.

"Well, Mount Rainier is more than fourteen thousand feet high, has some twenty-seven active glaciers on it and is one of the highest peaks in a range of mountains called the Western Cascades. It's a couple hours south of a big city called Seattle and on a clear day, people can sit in their office buildings and see this beautiful mountain. It's been used as the training grounds for some of the best mountaineers in the world because of the many active glaciers on the mountain. Billy, this mountain is alive and it never sleeps. It is magnificent, isn't it?"

Billy silently nodded his head. How did Papa know all this

stuff? He seemed so smart about everything. Suddenly, he thought about how he had blurted out "Can we go climb it when we're done making the puzzle?" and he felt embarrassed, but only for a fleeting moment. Really, Papa never made Billy feel bad about himself. In fact, Billy and Papa had adopted several rituals of their own, traditions if you will, and one of Billy's favorites was when he would ask a question and Papa, knowing full well that Billy probably already knew the answer, would repeat the question word-for-word back to him. Then they would laugh and recite in unison, "The only stupid question is the one you fail to ask."

"Well, Billy, let's get started. Making this puzzle should take us the better part of the day. That is, if you think we can finish it."

"Of course we can," cried Billy. "We'll finish it! We're up to the challenge."

Papa explained to Billy how they would go about assembling the five hundred-piece puzzle and they began by sorting out all of the pieces with straight edges on one side. These would be the pieces that would all fit together to make the border of the puzzle. In addition, there would be four pieces with two straight edges, these being the corner pieces of the puzzle. Once this was done, Papa told Billy that they should look at the picture on the puzzle box and try to determine where the pieces might fit in the border based upon the varying shades of color in the picture.

This was really fun for Billy since he had never made a jigsaw puzzle before, at least, not one with five hundred pieces! He felt safe and secure sitting next to Papa, who was so much older, filled with so much wisdom and whom he loved very much; and yet, they were both involved doing the same thing. Even better, as Billy started to find matches and fit pieces of the puzzle together, it made him think that this was something he was just as good at as any adult might be.

Late morning turned to afternoon. When they completed the border of the puzzle, they celebrated by taking a break for lunch. As they returned to the puzzle, the work got more tedious. The inside pieces didn't come together as quickly as the border had. At one point Papa commented, "If we don't finish this puzzle soon, Billy, all the snow on the mountain is going to melt!" Billy was getting a little tired of the slowing pace and was becoming a little frustrated with the whole process.

"Papa, do you think we will ever finish this puzzle?" Billy sighed.

"Of course we will, oh ye of little faith!" Papa shouted. Billy laughed at Papa's enthusiasm. "What we need is a little music to spur us onward and upward!"

Papa jumped from the couch and went to his stereo. One thing Papa did love was his music. He hardly ever turned on the television, but his stereo was one of his closest companions. It was a much older stereo system than the fancy digital-based sound system Billy's parents had recently bought. Papa's stereo consisted of a turntable with a plastic dust cover, a control unit, an amplifier and two oversized speakers. Papa didn't own any CDs, no, he was a "vinyl man." According to Papa, the only real music worth listening to was produced on vinyl. This opinion was just another one of Papa's firm beliefs that he felt the need to share with almost everyone he met.

Every time Papa turned on his stereo and played one of his vintage record albums, at least as far back as Billy could remember, Papa would say and do the same thing. It was like living the same moment over and over again, but Billy loved it. As Papa would place the vinyl record album on the turntable and carefully place the needle on the album, he would turn and look at Billy and say in a firm but gentle whisper, "Life should be put to music." For as long as Billy would live, these words, this simple philosophy, would serve as a constant reminder of the special, fun qualities that were so much a part of his grandfather.

And so, this puzzle-making endeavor would now be put to music. Papa cranked up the volume. It was a Glenn Miller album, and as *In the Mood* boomed from the stereo speakers, for the enjoyment of himself and his laughing, ten-year-old grandson, Papa grabbed a pillow off the couch and began dancing with it around the room. Billy laughed hysterically at Papa. "You're crazy, Papa!"

"If you knew how beautiful this pillow is that I'm dancing with, you'd know I'm not crazy, I'm in love," Papa responded as he twirled around the leather couch Billy was sitting on. Billy had seen his grandfather dance with this same pillow before and often wondered "who" the pillow was, but he never asked. He just enjoyed watching his grandfather sway back and forth to the music with the pillow in his arms. It was fun to see an adult play make believe.

As the music continued, Papa lowered the volume, sat back down on the couch with renewed energy and conviction, and got back to the task at hand. "Mount Rainier, today, you are mine!" he proclaimed in a loud voice. Billy looked at Papa, giggled, then laughed a little harder. Billy loved this man, his grandfather, and yes, the "little boy" in the man. Papa wasn't like most of the other adults Billy had met in his young life. There was something very different about him, something very special. Even with the rain and the change of plans, Billy's grandfather had found a way to make it a fun day for both himself and for his grandson.

It was getting to be later in the afternoon and the picture of Mount Rainier was, little by little, coming into view. The lake was completed, as were most of the trees in the foreground, and the mountain itself was now very discernible. Surely, they would finish the puzzle before dinner. One piece here, then another piece there, now turn that one to the right, fit the next one in, it was all coming together.

Suddenly, there were but a handful of pieces left in order to *finish* the puzzle. Papa grabbed a couple, Billy the other three or four, and they were fitting the final pieces together to complete the picture of Mount Rainier. Billy waited to place the last piece in the puzzle so that he could take credit for what was to be their shared moment of victory. As he placed the last piece in the puzzle, Billy clapped his hands and hollered, "Hooray, we have done it! It's *finished!*"

For some reason, Papa wasn't quite as jubilant. "Billy, I don't think we're finished," he said, a concerned look on his face. Billy looked again at their masterpiece. There in the upper right-hand corner of the picture was an irregular shaped hole where yet another puzzle piece needed to be inserted. It was part of the blue sky that made for such a wonderful backdrop for the majestic scene.

"Oh no, Papa, where is that piece?" Billy scrambled to the floor looking under the table and the leather couch. It was in neither place. He then looked behind the couch and then back on top of the coffee table where they had assembled the puzzle.

"Papa, it's not here, we're missing that piece. Without that piece, we can't say we really finished the puzzle. We can't finish the puzzle without the missing piece," Billy said in a desperate voice.

There was silence for a minute or two. The fire still crackling and popping in the room was the only sound to be heard until Papa broke the silence. "Interesting, very interesting."

"What do you mean, *interesting?* Papa, this is terrible! We worked all day on this puzzle and now because of some stupid missing piece, we can't even finish it." Billy was not a happy little boy and suddenly the excitement and fun of making the puzzle had turned to feelings of disappointment and failure. Billy was on the verge of tears. He did not like it when things didn't work out the way they were supposed to.

"No, Billy, I think this is good," Papa said in a comforting tone. "I think there's a lesson here for both of us."

"I don't want a lesson, Papa. I wanted to finish the puzzle," Billy responded.

"No, my good man, this is good. That missing piece is trying to teach us something, something about each of us; and if we think about it, the lesson here is probably far more important than actually finishing the puzzle," Papa said with a warm smile.

He went on. "You know, Billy, our lives are like puzzles. Our lives come together over time and paint a picture of what our lives look like, and the people in our lives are the 'pieces' that help make that picture. Think about it. Your mom and dad; me, your grandfather; your teachers at school; your friends; everyone that has come into your life in some way is part of your life — they are part of the puzzle. And, they are *all* important, every one of them. Now, some are certainly more important than others are, like your mom and dad, but every piece has its place in the puzzle."

Billy, listening intently behind a few stray tears, watched Papa as he pointed to the irregularly shaped hole in their picture of Mount Rainier that would have been home to the missing piece.

"Look at this picture of Mount Rainier, Billy. It's beautiful, absolutely magnificent. But no, it is not the finished picture we had hoped to complete. But, that's the way life is, too. We're never finished. I'm seventy-five years old but I'm not finished with my life. I look forward every day to learning new things, to reading books I've never read, to meeting new people, to seeing things I've never seen before. That's why I love this cottage and Mirror Lake and the four seasons that I live through every year. I learn from the seasons, from the changes in nature. That's what life is all about, *change,* and how we each choose to deal with it. And, as you and I are putting together our puzzles, our lives, we need to remember that who we are as people impacts other peoples' lives. We have our own puzzles but we are also part of *other* peoples' puzzles, too."

Billy had forgotten momentarily about the missing piece of the puzzle. Papa's message, his lesson, had captured Billy's full attention. He wanted to let Papa know that he was listening to his words. "You mean like when I play with my friends at school or at home, I'm actually part of their puzzle?"

"That's exactly what I'm saying!" Papa responded excitedly.

"And sometimes, without even knowing it, even when we don't come directly into someone's life, our actions, who we are, how we treat other people we come in contact with, can still impact their life, their puzzle, even though they may be total strangers to us."

"But, Papa, how is that?" This point confused Billy.

"Think about it, Billy. Look at our puzzle. That one missing piece impacts the whole picture. In this case it may only be part of the bright blue sky, but it definitely affects our picture. It leaves something out. Something is definitely missing from this puzzle. Every piece has its own purpose, a reason for being there. So, the way we interact with people we encounter in our daily lives may, in some way, affect how they touch other people in the course of their own lives. What I'm saying, Billy, is that we're connected to people we don't even know."

Billy was attentive but still somewhat confused. This was a little too abstract for a ten-year-old boy to comprehend. "Papa, I'm not sure I understand this part. How can I be connected to people I don't even know?"

Papa chuckled at Billy's honesty and seriousness. He rubbed the boy's fair hair and said, "Well, don't worry too much about that part. Let me share the most important point."

Billy sat up straight on the couch and perked up his ears. He didn't want to miss this point if it was really the most important point of Papa's lesson.

"Billy, every person, each of us, is a piece in a puzzle. We all have value. We all are very important to this world, and if you don't believe that, look at the puzzle we just made. Our missing piece is very important to the entire picture, just as every other piece of the puzzle is. That's because without it, something is missing! Our picture is not complete. Every piece of the puzzle is important, just as every person's life is important. Just as if I didn't have you in my life as my grandson, my goodness, my life's puzzle would have a huge missing piece!

Billy smiled when he heard these words. He looked up at his grandfather and in a soft, quiet tone, said, "Papa, I love you."

"Oh, William, William," Papa responded with a quiet chuckle, "I love you, too." He looked at his ten-year-old grandson and went on. "Billy, you will build a magnificent puzzle in your lifetime and I hope that someday, when you stand back and look at it, you'll remember which piece I am in your puzzle and the picture you have made of your life."

Billy reached up to hug his grandfather and felt the softness of his grandfather's old, worn flannel shirt against his cheek. He locked his arms around his grandfather's neck, and the fragrance of Old Spice After-Shave that had always been a part of Papa's cottage grew even stronger. He loved his grandfather and he felt safe and secure in his cottage, their special place. Hugging his grandfather on that cold and damp October afternoon, Billy realized, somehow, that this was a moment, a very special moment that he would remember and look back on throughout his entire life.

Papa got up from the couch and began to walk to the kitchen when he stopped in his tracks, cocked his head to the side, and turned around to look at Billy. "Hey, I've got a great idea."

"Oh no, not another puzzle!" Billy said as he wiped his forearm across his brow.

"No, no, nothing like that," Papa said with a laugh. "I think we ought to do something special to remember this day and the things we learned together as a result of the missing piece."

"Well, what's your great idea, Papa?" Billy asked.

Papa responded, "I think we should each take one piece from the puzzle as a keepsake to remind us of what we both learned today from the missing piece. That way, every day, we'll have a little reminder when we each look at our piece from the puzzle. You can keep your piece from the puzzle in a special, secret place, or just carry it in your pocket. But, every time you look at it, it will remind you how important you are and how important each and every person is. So, you can pick one piece and I will pick one piece and we'll keep these as souvenirs from our special day together."

Billy liked this idea and now looked at all the pieces in the puzzle from which he was going to select his special souvenir. His little fingers reached to the center of the picture and he fumbled with the connected pieces of the puzzle until he had loosened the piece he wanted. Billy took the piece that had the very summit of Mount Rainier on it.

"So, you went for the summit," Papa said. "Any reason why?"

"Yes," declared Billy. "Someday, I'm going to climb Mount Rainier and when I get to the summit, I'm going to take this piece of the puzzle out of my pocket and think of you, Papa, and this special day we have had together. I am going to do that, Papa, and I mean it, too!"

Papa laughed. "William, you are a very determined young

man. That would be quite an accomplishment if you were to climb Mount Rainier and to know that you'd think of me when you did it ... well, I would be honored."

"C'mon, Papa, pick your piece," Billy said.

Papa looked at the puzzle as he pinched his chin between his thumb and forefinger. He was giving his selection some serious thought. "Well, let me see. This is a big decision, you know." He paused a moment longer. "Aha, there it is!"

Papa's fingers reached for one of the blue pieces of sky that would have been directly over the summit of Mount Rainier in the picture. "This is the one I want."

"Papa, why did you pick such a boring piece? Yours is nothing but blue sky. Why did you pick that one?" Billy asked.

"Well, from my perspective, this is the best piece I could ever pick. First, blue is my favorite color. Second, it's from the sky. Whenever I have had troubles in my life, I have prayed about them and looked to the heavens for the help and courage that I needed. So, I find comfort whenever I look up into the sky. And last, when you finally are old enough to climb Mount Rainier, I'll probably be somewhere up there in the heavens looking down on you. When you reach the summit and pull your piece of the puzzle out of your pocket to remember me, I'll be up there looking down and holding my piece of the puzzle in my hand, thinking of you."

"Hey Papa, do you know what I'm thinking?" Billy asked.

"Maybe, but I'm not sure. What?" Papa inquired.

"Well, all this talk and stuff has been neat, but I'm starving!"

Papa laughed and reached to tickle Billy's mid-section. "You're right Billy, I've gotten carried away with all this talk. Let's see, still raining outside, hmmm, I think this calls for a trip into town, pizza for dinner and then a movie. How's that sound?"

"Yahoo!" Billy shouted with glee. "That sounds great."

"Well, go wash up and let's get ready to go," Papa said.

Billy scurried off to the bathroom and as the door shut, Papa looked down at the puzzle with the now three missing pieces. He smiled to himself, looked at his missing piece of sky and put it in his pocket as he slowly got up from the leather couch. He walked to the kitchen where he leaned on the kitchen sink, resting his weary arms on the counter and looked out the window through the trees to the tranquil Mirror Lake. He loved this view and this place. He thought about his life and all he had — and had not — done with it.

He thought about his parents, long dead and gone, and his one brother whom he never heard from. He thought about his loving wife of forty-seven years who had died so suddenly, so unfairly, as she was hit by a car while crossing the street. He thought about his only son, Billy's dad, his daughter-in-law Sarah, a wonderful woman, though a little too strong-willed for his taste, and he thought about Billy, his only grandson.

He was seventy-five years old now, and if this were the autumn of his life, clearly, most of the leaves had fallen from the tree. He was getting older and he felt it, even though he did not like to admit it. What had he done with his life? What did his puzzle really look like? He'd never really thought about it that way until today; life as a puzzle with the people that come into our lives as the pieces. Funny, how a ten-year-old, a child, can give you such a different perspective on everything. Generally speaking, he was happy and felt like he had lived a full life, but he wanted more. He wasn't ready to say good-bye just yet — not to this place, this life, not to his grandson, Billy.

"Okay, Papa, I'm ready," Billy's voice chirped as he skipped his way into the kitchen. He had washed his hands and had attempted to comb his hair, even though his part was in three different places.

Papa got a kick out of Billy's efforts. "My goodness, aren't you the handsome devil? Are we going for pizza and a movie or to find the ladies?"

Billy sheepishly grinned and looked at the floor feeling his cheeks flush a bit. Papa grabbed his car keys and said, "Let's go" and they headed out the door. The rain had stopped. It was almost dark now with the sky a deep dark blue and the first star of the night appearing in the east.

"There's Venus!" shouted Billy. This was another piece of minutiae that Papa had taught Billy; that the first star visible at night wasn't a star at all, but was really the planet Venus. Of course, the moral of this teaching was, don't believe everything you see. Even our eyes can lie to us on occasion.

"Yes, there she is," Papa answered. He stopped and looked up at the autumn sky. It was damp and cold and he felt the chill of winter approaching. He wondered just for a fleeting moment what it would be like to live in the sky and look down on it all?

"C'mon Papa, I'm hungry!" The silence of the night was

broken by the cries for food from an impatient and hungry ten-year-old. Yes, this was the world he was still a part of, his reality for this day.

He looked over his shoulder to the lake and thought to himself, Oh how I do love this view, this place, this life.

Yes, this was a good place to be and this had been a very special day.

Maybe, just maybe, tomorrow would be even better.

PART II

Our Search for Security

Chapter 1

ॐ

The Security Blanket, Is There Such a Thing?

A boy and his grandfather spend a rainy, autumn day together making a puzzle. It makes for a nice story.

The ten-year-old, a mere child, loves his grandfather and the cottage that he lives in almost as much. It's the *perfect place* in that little boy's mind, regardless of the season; and with all the wonderful aromas and the special warmth that comes from his grandfather's love as much as the crackling fire in the fireplace, he has no reason to be afraid when he is there. It is a *safe* place.

He is also the center of his grandfather's attention for the day. He is doing something that is "fun." With pizza for dinner and an evening at the movies to end the day, why shouldn't he be happy? My guess would be that when he hugged his grandfather after completing their puzzle (as much as they could, remember, they never did *finish* the puzzle), Billy felt as safe and secure and happy as any child can feel. At that moment, there was no other person or place in the world he would rather be. Wouldn't it be nice if every child could have this kind of experience, this sense of security, at least once in their life?

On the other hand, how does the grandfather feel about his life? He is seventy-five years old, feeling his age and growing weary. He is living by himself in a place he loves but it is a place that cannot love him back. One can assume that he is alone, living most of his waking hours by himself when his grandson or other company is not there. He still has some "little boy" left in him, which is an admirable quality, but he is also stubborn and opinionated about certain subjects. And, he is scarred from the traumas and experiences that have been part of his puzzle, his life.

The grandfather does, however, have this uplifting, positive outlook on life: a belief that there is always hope for a better tomorrow. We see this in his attitude throughout the day and in the positive message he shares with his grandson regarding the missing piece of the puzzle. His ability to take a negative circumstance and find good in what is perceived as negative is a very powerful attribute to have. He accepts the reality of the moment; but then, he transcends the perceived negative with a very enlightening and inspiring message that speaks to the value and importance of every person and how we all are connected to one another. Whether it is the rainy weather that forces a change in plans for the day or the missing piece that thwarts their efforts to complete the puzzle, the grandfather finds good in every circumstance. What a wonderful quality to possess.

However, late in the story as the day is ending, he has a brief moment of solitude and introspection as he stares quietly out his kitchen window and he asks himself questions about his own life and everything he has or has not done. He can speak the words and give the lesson to his grandson, but has he lived the lesson himself? At this point in his life, is he *really* the person he wants to be? Is he *where* he wants to be? Is he truly at peace with himself? These are questions we all ask ourselves at some point in our lives. Why is that?

We, as Americans, are fortunate to live in the greatest country in the world. We are blessed to be where we can exercise the many freedoms we enjoy and pursue whatever it is we choose to do, ultimately enjoying a lifestyle far greater than that which exists in many parts of the world. We have advanced technology that allows us to communicate with whomever we want at any time of day, from any place. Medical research also has made significant advances, discovering new treatments and cures for disease, allowing us to live longer, more productive lives. This is a great country and we have much to be thankful for. But, for some reason, it's not enough.

In many respects, as a society, we are and have been unhappy people and in some cases, unhappy to the point of being angry and filled with rage. This is scary. In many respects, the events of September 11 have altered this state of mind and brought out the best in us. We now live with a renewed sense of patriotism, and are more caring toward one another. We have mourned and grieved together over a common loss and it has bonded us and united us like never before. This is an interesting phenomenon, and personally, one that I hope never ends. I would like to believe that we are all better people today as a result of what we experienced on September 11, both as individuals and as a country. But, why did it take such a devastating tragedy to arouse these feelings of national pride and good will? Why weren't we like this on September 10 and in the days, weeks, months and years prior to the terrorist attacks?

In many respects, we were our own worst enemy. Having enough was never enough. We just were not very happy with our lives. So, in many cases, we chose to live our lives excessively. As a people we were undisciplined: eating too much, drinking too much and often spending beyond our means. Our job was never good enough, and even if it was, we probably complained that we were not being paid enough or were under appreciated by our employer. We were also discontented with our personal lives, either because of a failing marriage or problems with some sort of relationship we were involved in. Really, you could characterize a lot of people in our society as being pretty unhappy.

In many respects, much of this unhappiness is still present in our lives. Some things have not changed. We can find crises in our homes and in our schools, and it even affects our attitudes about the more trivial matters of life. We have become more demanding, especially as consumers of products and services, and we are ready to litigate against one another at the drop of a hat if we think we can make a buck doing so. Time is more precious than ever before. No one seems to have enough hours in a day to get everything done and "speed to market" is the mantra of the day for business people. We have better technology and communication tools than ever before in the history of mankind, yet we may be the worst communicators to ever live on the planet! Yes, this is our world today. It is hectic, fast-paced, constantly changing, and filled with never-ending challenges for each and every one of us. And, if this truly is our world, the one we wake up to every morning and live through until the next morning, one must ask him- or herself, "Where does one go to find some sense of security in this world of ours?" Maybe the question should be, "Can we ever really find security at all?"

The search for security is a never-ending process and one that we all seek in our own way. From the time we leave the comfort, warmth and darkness of our mother's womb, of that *perfect place,* we find ourselves seeking some form of security in the outside world. Most of us as infants developed an attachment to a certain blanket, stuffed animal or toy, our security blanket. This object, whatever it may have been, became a constant companion that went with us everywhere, from room-to-room or even on trips outside our home. It was the replacement, the substitute, for the safety and security we experienced subconsciously in the womb. It became the one thing we could count on in the outside world that was consistent and always available to us. If everything else in the world went wrong, give us our security blanket, and maybe a thumb to suck on, and the world was right again.

As we grew older, our efforts to find this sense of security did not come as easily. We no longer were able to find our security through a physical object and our efforts became much more cerebral. Of course, we wanted a safe and comfortable place to live, but more importantly, we wanted to be accepted by others, to be successful in some way, shape or form. As we completed our high-school years, we sprung from adolescence into young adulthood and were filled with dreams and ambitions that would define what we intended to make of our lives. Mostly, we were optimistic, believing that we would have complete, productive, fulfilling lives avoiding the pitfalls that might challenge our feelings of security. We would be safe, successful and secure.

Unfortunately, there were no such guarantees and many of us were forced to deal with the realities of life in today's world: broken marriages, strained relationships, conflicts with our children, financial struggles and absolutely no guarantees in the workplace regardless of title and position. It wasn't supposed to be like this, or so we thought. What many of us looked forward to in adulthood, what we thought would be our "walk in the park" so to speak, instead has transformed itself into a tightrope walk over a lion's den. One might ask, "Is it really that bad or is this just our *perception* of life today as we compare it with our past, with simpler times?"

Somehow, we all would still like to find that security blanket for ourselves and along with it, those warm, safe feelings that Billy felt at his grandfather's cottage. Some of us seek those feelings of security through education and higher learning. The thought process here is that if we advance ourselves intellectually and earn certain degrees for our efforts, we will have everything we need in life to solve our problems and, in turn, find that sense of security we long for. For others, it may come from our endeavors in our professional lives or from the accumulation of material possessions and wealth, adhering to the philosophy espoused by the well-known bumper sticker, "He Who Dies with the Most Toys Wins."

Then again, some people are much more focused on the relationships in their lives and the quality of those relationships. For these people, personal relationships make up the very fabric of their lives in their search for security. For others, the focus may be a single relationship — marriage — and this is where they hope to find their feelings of security. For others, becoming a parent and taking on the role of nurturing, caring, teaching and loving a child becomes the place where they hope to find their security, a security that says we do matter, that we are important and that we are needed.

Finally, some people may attempt to find their sense of security through their individual actions and activities. Whatever it is they choose to do — skydive, adventure racing, climb mountains, hang glide, run marathons — in "going to the edge" they hope to come away with a deeper understanding of themselves and, in the course of that journey, maybe find some sense of security.

In any number of ways, we as individuals would like to find our place in this world. This place is not a destination, but a state of mind. It is a consciousness, an attitude, an understanding of oneself that fulfills us and assures us that we are okay. It is what confirms to us that our life has meaning and that we matter. And, if we are lucky enough to ever find this place, this will be where we find our sense of security and a certain inner peace that says who I am and the life I have lived really did count for something.

This is what we will examine in the second section of this book; how each of us, as individuals, seeks to find our own sense of security.

Defining Security:
Do We Know What It Is We Are Looking For?

Maybe the logical place to start is by addressing the question, "What is security?" By dictionary definition, security is (1) safety, (2) freedom from worry, (3) something given as a pledge for payment, (4) a bond or stock, (5) protection. What I have been referring to in the first several pages of this section are definitions 1, 2 and 5, safety, freedom from worry, and protection.

What is *safe* in our world today? Is there anywhere in this world today where we can think of ourselves as being absolutely safe? We can make our homes safer places to live, we can practice safety in how we operate the motor vehicles we drive; we can in a sense, make wiser choices in an attempt to ensure our safety. But, we can never *guarantee* our safety. Anyone who has ever climbed a mountain knows that one of the basic tenets, or truths, on the mountain is that you can manage risk but you can never really eliminate it. The same is true in all aspects of our life. There are no guarantees.

Of course, if we are going to try to ensure safety in our lives, we must jump to the last definition, *protection*. Protection can come in many forms. It can be the physical barriers or the fortresses that we construct to protect ourselves. Protection also can be the metal detectors we walk through at the airport, detecting the presence of metal that might indicate a firearm or explosive device being smuggled onboard a commercial airliner. Protection could be the security systems we install in our homes to keep our loved ones and us safe from unwanted intruders. While all of these forms of protection refer to our physical well-being, we sometimes, even consciously, play mind games with ourselves as a form of mental protection that keeps us mentally safe.

More than protection, these mental tricks we play on ourselves are delusions. This can come in the form of simple *denial* where we refuse to acknowledge certain realities that exist in our lives, such as our own shortcomings and insecurities. Then again, it may take the form of the *rationalizations* that we use in our everyday life to justify in our minds why we choose to act in a particular way. All of us are guilty of doing these things from time to time. More than a form of protection, they are part of a defense mechanism that keeps us from having to deal with the parts of our own reality that we would just as soon not deal with.

However, while real protection in the physical sense plays a role in managing the risk in our lives, there is no *perfect* protection. That's the reality of what we are dealing with in today's world. There is nothing that is totally safe, and there is no perfect protection. So, that being the case, one must ponder this very painful possibility: If there is no absolute safety and no perfect protection in this world, then could there ever be freedom from worry?

This is a sobering question to ask oneself because if we decide that there is no freedom from worry one must then ask, "How then can I ever truly be happy in life?" Think about it. When was the last time you were happy when you were also busy worrying about something? If you were to walk around with constant worry, with fear locked in your heart and mind and soul, could you ever really find any happiness in life?

Whereas safety and protection dealt more with the physical aspect of our life, with the reality of our existence, freedom from worry deals totally with our state of mind, an attitude, a conscious choice we can make. We can choose to worry or we can choose to go about life, making what we believe to be wise and good choices, and not worry. It is that simple. This issue, freedom from worry deals much more with the deeper meaning of security: to find an inner peace.

While we cannot control circumstances or some of the events that occur in our lives, we can control our thoughts, our attitude and how we respond to such events as they occur, just as Billy's grandfather did in the story. Thus, the choice is left to each of us. We can either choose to fill our minds with fears and doubts and then worry about them, or we can deal with our own reality, accept it for what it is, and move on without burdening ourselves mentally with worrisome thoughts. So, of all the definitions we have examined, freedom from worry is the one definition of security that we can achieve in our lives, if we so choose.

For some reason, however, we don't see this so much as a choice we can make in our lives, but instead, something we must achieve or earn through hard work. For example, take a person who pours themselves into career endeavors, hoping to achieve a certain level of financial success, status and power that they believe will give them the security they are looking for. They may succeed in achieving many of their goals and as a result, believe they are safe and secure because of those successes. However, when this person least expects it, WHAM! The company he or she works for is acquired and suddenly, they are notified that their position is being eliminated. The past successes, the titles, count for nothing. They do not guarantee anything in life. And so, our friend may find him- or herself, disappointed, disillusioned and struggling because of certain expectations they might have had. Surprised by the events, he or she laments, "I thought this would give me the security I was looking for. Where is my security blanket now?"

I will never forget an experience I had several years ago when travelling on a business trip. I was in Washington, D.C., and it was a bitter cold winter night with the temperature hovering just above the single digits. Being somewhat of an adventurous individual, I decided to brave the elements and go for an evening run. It was a good, invigorating run that took me by many of Washington's historical landmarks and buildings. Snow crunching under my feet with every step, the cold air had numbed my cheeks and frozen the sweat on my eyebrows. As I approached the backside of the White House nearing the end of my five-mile run, I saw a strangely shaped figure in the street up ahead of me. As I drew closer, I literally stopped in my tracks. It was a man huddled in a cardboard box that had obviously been used for packaging some type of household appliance, maybe a washing machine or a stove. This man had three sides of the box wrapped over and around his body. And, in an attempt to stay warm, had strategically placed himself over a manhole cover that was spewing steam from the sewers below. There, in full view of the White House was this homeless man, fighting to stay warm in his cardboard hut on a bitterly cold winter night. I asked myself, where was his security blanket? Why was he, why should anybody, be forced to live a life such as this?

Later, as I stood in my steaming hot shower at the Marriott Hotel, I could not stop thinking about that man, the sight of him hovering over a sewer in an attempt to find his own warmth. I wondered who was that man and where did his story begin? What choices had he made in his life that somehow, tragically, had put him in that predicament? What would it really be like to be a homeless person in today's world? How does someone survive like that? That night, that man and his cardboard box made an impression that would be with me the rest of my life. To this day I still think about him and the fact that on that night, I failed to do anything about his circumstances. What was I thinking? Where was my head? More importantly, where was my heart?

We all want security in our lives and we seek it in many different ways. However, if we are looking for guarantees, we are sure to be disappointed. Regardless of what we accomplish or achieve in life, in an instant, our world may be transformed from one of false security to one of complete turmoil. What is even more surprising, confusing — and unfortunately, all too common — is that even if the turmoil does not come into our lives many of us still feel a certain emptiness or void even though we have achieved certain goals.

Security and Identity — Not One in the Same

Maybe we aren't struggling with issues of security as much as we are issues that relate to establishing one's *identity*. Identity is not so much about freedom from worry as it is about character and individuality, about who we really are. It is important for each of us to establish our own identity because this is where our self-worth comes from. We need to understand who we are and be able to honestly assess and accept our strengths and weaknesses. We need to set goals for ourselves, extend ourselves, grow and learn. If we do these things, and if we choose to be honest with ourselves in making our personal assessment, we begin to approach an understanding that life is so much bigger, so much more, than just achieving. Why do I say this?

I have had the good fortune of crossing paths with some remarkable people in my lifetime, people who have accomplished some extraordinary things, traveled the world and seen things that many of us may never get to see. By most standards, the majority of us would consider these individuals to be very successful. These are the kind of people many of us might look at enviously, and say, "Boy, now there's someone who's really got it made." However, when you do get to know some of these individuals and who they *really* are, aside from their many wonderful achievements, the truth is they are not any different than anyone else. They have their own set of worries and ask themselves the same questions that you and I might ask ourselves.

The truth is, there is no *real* security in life for any of us, at least not as it exists in the form of safety or protection in the perfect sense. At best, security is a temporary state, an illusion, a mirage that may bring a false sense of hope and peace that our world is protected and can never be derailed by outside forces. In reality, maybe the best we can do is strive to be positive people, people who make the choice and have the attitude necessary to realize the freedom from worry we have discussed. This may be the closest we ever come to finding security in our lifetime.

Certainly, each of us needs to have a sense of purpose in our lives, our own mission statement if you will, that guides our thoughts and actions. But as part of this goal, we must strive for something more than just achievement in our lives, something that gives our lives real meaning and purpose. While we might establish our identities and our individuality by what we accomplish, we cannot, and should not, expect those accomplishments to fill the void in our lives or eliminate the feelings of worry that so many of us have. At the end of the day, accomplishments alone are not enough.

As we look back at our story, we might ask ourselves, "What did Billy and his grandfather have at the end of their day together?"

One might guess that Billy certainly had a sense of belonging based upon the love and understanding his grandfather showed him throughout the day. We might also surmise that he even had a healthier self-esteem based upon his contributing to the making of the puzzle and how his grandfather had made Billy the focus of the day.

I do know one thing Billy had at the end of his day; no, make that, two things. One, he had a wonderful memory of a very special day spent with his grandfather. His memory was one that could, and would, last a lifetime and that nobody could ever take away from him. And two, he had a piece from a puzzle with the picture of the summit of Mount Rainier on it.

Sometimes, we look too deep; we get lost in our search for meaning. Billy knew what he had and he didn't have to look for it. He felt it. His little fingers felt the piece from the puzzle in his pocket and the other things he had, he felt in his heart. Which brings us to one more question:

What did Billy's grandfather have at the end of the day?

Chapter 2

Searching for Security through Learning and the Accumulation of Knowledge

For a ten-year-old, Billy is a pretty bright little boy. We can guess that he's in the fourth or fifth grade. It is important to Billy that his grandfather knows how smart he is. This is why he is so quick to inform his grandfather that he knows where the state of Washington is when his grandfather is telling him the location of Mount Rainier. And so it is for most young children in their early years of formal education. They want to learn. They want to share what they have learned or accomplished in their day. By sharing what they have learned and then getting the positive affirmation from a parent or a grandparent, someone they love, they feel a sense of security, of well-being. The child actually associates this feeling of well-being, of security, with the acknowledgement of what they have learned.

As for Billy's grandfather, we can't say for sure how smart he is, but he obviously has knowledge of certain matters and an attitude that learning, in and of itself, should be an ongoing process. He sees the whole world as his classroom and he tells his grandson that he even learns from nature, from the changes he sees in the seasons. His attitude about life and people and how we are all connected makes him a bit of a philosopher and his appreciation for music might even give us a hint that he has an appreciation for the arts as well. We don't know if he holds a high school diploma or has a Ph.D., but his respect for learning is honorable. More than being intelligent, he is wise.

The quest for learning and knowledge is as old as the existence of man and in many cases, it has become a source of security for many. Going back to the days of the ancient Greek philosophers, a sound mind (an educated mind) in a sound body was considered to be an admirable virtue. In history, the educated man has always been held in high esteem and to seek higher learning, to attain knowledge, has always been considered a just and noble pursuit.

The successful completion of one's formal education, however, holds no actual promise or guarantee of security or the assurance of a better life. Learning, the accumulation of knowledge alone, bears no fruit for the individual. The quality of one's life, the success that one achieves in his or her lifetime, is really a function of how well the individual applies what they have learned. It is the application of knowledge, the choices that we make and yes, probably some luck and good timing along the way, that determines the actual quality that one finds in life.

As parents, we all want our children to be well educated because we believe in our hearts that education, or knowledge, holds the promise of a better life for them. Personally speaking, I am one of these parents. I have always believed this, but not for the reason that it might necessarily allow for greater financial success in life.

Learning, simply put, is an investment one makes in oneself. Striving to become more knowledgeable about our world can only have positive results for us. It can never be a losing proposition. Education is our basis for understanding our world and each other. In the process of learning new things (in a formal education environment, especially at the college or professional level), the individual learns much about life itself. From these extended courses of study, one learns the value of perseverance and patience and develops the attitude necessary to help overcome adversity later in life. It enables us to grow in many, many ways and, as part of this process, come away with greater self-confidence and self-esteem for what we accomplish. The value that this kind of learning experience can potentially have for an individual over the course of a lifetime cannot be quantified. It is immeasurable.

However, if one chooses to seek their security through their academic pursuits, they may find themselves filled with feelings of emptiness and disappointment later in life. Why is this?

Well, as we have discussed, the accumulation of knowledge, the earning of degrees, while noble in pursuit, brings with it no guarantee of success. For example, while a degree from a respected university may open a door, it does not guarantee good performance or any level of success that might be attained in the workplace. Certain attributes may have been developed or learned in the educational process, but in the workplace, it becomes a function of how well one applies what has been learned that determines how one performs. Also, if the student decides to become an educator by profession, he or she will go through an interesting transformation. Over time, the eager, young, educated scholar grows to become an older and wiser academician, and with that transformation comes the realization of how little they really do know. It is an interesting phenomenon. The more we learn, the more we realize how much there is that we don't know.

We will never know everything. No one has all the answers and we never will. This is a simple truth. So, while simply accumulating knowledge can never hold the secret to finding security in this life, there is and always will be tremendous value in maintaining a spirit of learning, especially when it occurs outside of the formal education process.

This is the kind of learning that Billy's grandfather was all about. Billy's grandfather believed that we never stop learning, that the whole world is our classroom and that we have opportunities all around us to learn every day. If we choose to take advantage of these opportunities, then we become what I like to call a student of life.

A student of life is someone who enjoys learning new things for the sake of learning and for the new perspective they gain every time they learn something new. When we embrace this attitude, we constantly are looking for opportunities to learn and we never get tired of learning new things. We can make these discoveries wherever we are — at home, in school, at work — the opportunities are everywhere. We can learn from the changes we see in Mother Nature's miracles as the seasons change, just as Billy's grandfather did. As adults, we probably can learn something from the innocence of a five-year-old. The lessons are there for us every day, all around us, if only we'll take the time to slow down a little and open our eyes.

If there is to be any security found in our efforts to learn and acquire knowledge, it may come from the realization of two things: one, no matter how much knowledge we attain, we will never know everything, and two, we should never stop learning. There are, and always will be, new things to learn.

I do not believe that we were ever meant to explain away everything, to have all the answers. We need to understand that it is okay to ponder, to wonder, to ask questions about those issues outside of ourselves as well as those that deal with our innermost feelings. When we do this, we begin to truly understand and appreciate how magnificent our world is and also how special each and every one of us is.

More than knowledgeable, Billy's grandfather was wise. As a student of life, he looked for new opportunities to learn wherever and whenever he could. In doing so, he had discovered something that very few people ever grasp in their lifetime...that life can be a much richer and more rewarding experience when we come to accept who *we really are* and how little about this magnificent world we really do know. This wasn't part of any course curriculum, just something he'd picked up along the way during his seventy-five years on the planet.

Billy learned a lot from his grandfather. Maybe we could, too.

Chapter 3

❧

Searching for Our Security in the Workplace

In our story, we don't know what Billy's grandfather did for a living. It is never revealed to us, never mentioned in any way. But, do we care? Should we care? What we do know is that he is a loving, caring individual who is somewhat opinionated and, yes, has a sense of humor. He likes to have fun and maybe more than anything else, he is wise. Although, we never really know what he does (or did) for a living, he is a very likable, lovable person. It is easy to see that regardless of his professional accomplishments or lack thereof, it certainly doesn't make any difference to his grandson. Billy loves his grandfather and everything about him, even the place where he lives. I guess there is a certain beauty in his simplicity.

It is interesting that so many of us are consumed by what we do for a living. Much of this fixation, this mentality of total commitment to our career endeavors has to do with our search for security. After all, this is largely how many of us, especially men, define ourselves and measure our success in life, by what we do professionally.

Many of us justify our dedication and the time commitment we make to our professional lives with the reasoning that how hard we work is a direct reflection of how much we really love our family. After all, it is through our hard work and dedication that we provide financially for our families. This is how we explain and rationalize in our minds the long hours we put in at the office away from those who are most important to us.

Some of us were taught and believe that if we work harder than the other guy, those we compete with, we will win in the end. This was ingrained in my thinking as I look back on my days as an athlete and a coach. For me, this mentality was, and still is, a very clear and simple philosophy: You worked harder, you were in *better shape* than your opponent; you worked harder, you were *better prepared* than your opponent; you worked harder, you were *mentally tougher* than your opponent; you worked harder than your opponent, *you WIN!* I practiced this credo; I lived it; and I did achieve a certain level of success living by this philosophy both in athletics and in my professional life.

However, this "Type A," intense, never-say-die behavior can take a toll on the individual. Most of us who live by this credo are mentally exhausted from our work day when we arrive at home. We push hard at the office, drive ourselves day-in and day-out and tend to have very high, sometimes unrealistic, expectations of ourselves. We also probably do not get enough sleep or take care of ourselves the way we should. And we do it all, for what? The next promotion? A new title? A few more bucks the government is going to take a good portion of anyway?

I was reminded of this kind of work ethic that has driven so many of us to succeed one evening while watching an excerpt on ESPN. It highlighted the weekly work schedule of a certain head football coach in the NFL. I watched the excerpt with real interest because, quite frankly, I really like this coach. He has passion for what he does and for his players and you can see it when he's on the sidelines during a game. He also is, and has been, a real student of the game and he takes his profession very seriously. I admire that. Well, in the course of this excerpt, the coach acknowledged that he only needs four to five hours of sleep a night and that he tries to put the other eighteen to twenty hours a day into his work. He actually arrives at the office by 4 A.M. every day to start his film breakdown, practice organization, etc., and on some occasions, has been known to sleep in his office instead of going home for the night.

Wow! — I thought to myself — now that is real dedication. I like this guy! I like his toughness, that certain "macho" quality and I believe he is a great coach. But — I had to ask myself — will this really guarantee him the success and security he is looking for? What if his players don't execute on the field? Worse yet, what if he doesn't get the best talent (players) to work with — will he ever achieve his goal of winning a Super Bowl? What will his eighteen- to twenty-hour days have bought him then? Peace of mind in knowing that he, personally, did everything humanly possible in coaching his team so they might win a Super Bowl? And then what? What is one left with when the ride is over? Will he look back on his life and wonder what he might have missed because of all those eighteen to twenty hour workdays?

Ah ... these are the choices we make that paint the picture of our lives.

Over the past twenty to twenty-five years, many women have made the choice to enter the workplace and in doing so, changed the fabric of the American family. Many women have decided that they did not want to stay at home as their mothers had done. This is understandable. The world has changed, and there is far more opportunity for women in the workplace today than there was in the past. Today, more women are college educated, have advanced degrees, and have clearly proven themselves in the workplace. Women have found success in industry, medicine, government, journalism, higher education and the like. In many respects, women tend to be more driven than their male counterparts in the workplace. I say this because they have succeeded, in many cases against the odds, in a man's world. Their success stories are many and no one can deny that women have proven themselves to be very capable, strong performers. But, these achievements have had a downside, too.

Because many women have taken on greater responsibilities in conjunction with their professional endeavors, the stereotypes that were often applied to men and their obsession with their lives in the workplace now can be applied to many women. Where men often sought their identities and much of who they were through their professional endeavors, now much of the same can be said of many women in the workplace. In addition, while men were often maligned for their ambivalence to family matters in comparison to their professional responsibilities, this also has become an issue for many professional women today.

Many men and women today commit themselves to their jobs and their professional responsibilities over their home lives, and this sometimes happens without them ever realizing it. This commitment may show up in the form of business travel that regularly starts to cut into weekend family time, requiring mom or dad to leave home on Sunday afternoon or evening to begin their work week. Then again, it may be a more drastic situation as when the entire family is forced to relocate to a different part of the country because of a promotion that promises more responsibility, a better title, more hours (and hassles) on the job, oh yeah, and a few more bucks. Is this wrong? Maybe, maybe not. Every person's situation is their own to deal with; only they can decide what is right or wrong based upon their own circumstances. But as I pointed out, this is often done, almost unconsciously, because they believe that their work effort is a direct reflection of how much they really do love their family. That is their justification.

Complicating the workplace issue even more for women is the fact that many professional women today are psychologically and emotionally torn between two very different lifestyles: One is their professional life and the other one is the choice to stay at home and raise a family. This can be an extremely difficult decision for some women, and yet for others may be very clear-cut. In some cases, the woman may say, "I can have and do both!" in which case I say, "Never argue with a determined woman." I must say that my experience has been that women, in most cases, do a better job of balancing their professional lives with their personal lives than men do. However, there is no doubt that they are now faced with some of the same trappings that men were once accused of. We might even find that many men *and* women are asking themselves the same question, "Is what I do for a living who I really am?"

I think about this question and my thoughts turn to my mother's business career. I say this because of an experience I had that was related to her and how she carried herself in her business life. My mother, Anne, had essentially been a housewife and mom to her three sons all of her adult life. But as we grew older, she had more time on her hands and was introduced to the world of selling cosmetics door-to-door by a friend. Intrigued by the opportunity to work out of our home part-time and make money, she decided to take a shot at it. You guessed it; my mother became an Avon Lady.

She was given a territory that had never produced very well, but she was new to the business and probably a little naïve and didn't really concern herself with how the territory had performed in the past. Instead, she just did what the people at Avon had told her to do. She began calling on the homes in her territory, going door-to-door, introducing herself as the new Avon Lady. She made some progress and then thought if she called on some of the businesses in her territory (a couple of banks, a bakery, etc.), selling to the employees, she might be able to increase her sales.

Not a bad strategy…and she began to have success, both door-to-door and with her new commercial accounts. Long story short: she ended up working that particular territory for twenty-one years and maybe even more impressive, she achieved and exceeded her quota in twenty of those twenty-one years.

She never talked much about her sales successes. Oh, maybe she would occasionally mention what a huge order she was going to have for the Christmas season or something about the new jewelry that Avon was going to introduce. She was very proud of the company she represented and their products and was never ashamed to tell people that she was an Avon Lady even though she never had, to my knowledge, even a business card with her name on it.

I really believe her success with Avon was very important to her and something she was proud of even though she never made it a topic of conversation. Clearly, she was still a mom first and that was where her priorities were. That was clear to all of us. I was always proud of her, who she was as a person and for her accomplishments with Avon, but it wasn't until her death in 1991 that I learned what an impact she had had in the workplace as an Avon Lady.

She died rather suddenly. Doctors had found two brain tumors and complications during a biopsy procedure led to hemorrhaging in the brain that left her totally incapacitated. She contracted pneumonia while she was in the hospital and died five weeks following the procedure, at a very young seventy years of age.

Hundreds of friends in our community came to the funeral home to pay their respects. In fact, the crowds had been so heavy at one point that local police had to be called to direct traffic in and out of the parking lot. With the visitation hours winding down, I suggested to my two brothers, John and Rick, that they go home and that my mom's only sister, Bess, and I would hold the fort for the remaining two hours. This made sense since our kids were restless and we had other relatives and friends in town for the funeral.

About five minutes before the visitation hours ended, two people I had never seen before walked into the room and up to my mother's casket. It was a couple, an older man and a woman. I assumed a father and either a daughter or maybe a niece. The man was probably mid-sixties, silver-haired, dressed in casual navy-blue slacks, a wrinkled golf shirt and a tan windbreaker jacket. The woman, who was probably mid to late twenties, was wearing a black, tightly fitted dress with black high heels. She was, excuse my poor choice of words for this occasion, absolutely drop-dead gorgeous! Who were these two people, these two strangers?

I just sat in my chair and watched them for a minute. They stood alone by my mother's casket, and then, the man began to shake and he broke into a heavy sob. His entire body shook and the woman at his side grabbed his arm. I stepped forward to offer some assistance. I handed the man a Kleenex and once he had composed himself, I helped him and the young lady over to a couch where we could sit down. I introduced myself as my mother's middle son and asked the two people, "Do I know you? Should I know you?"

The man looked me in the eye, shook my hand, apologized for his loss of composure and then told me this story. "Your mom," he began, "was our Avon Lady. But, more importantly, my wife, who passed away very suddenly just four weeks ago, considered your mom to be her very best friend."

He then went on to explain how his wife had died very suddenly from a heart attack and how he was so concerned and hurt when my mom had not shown up at the funeral home for her wake or for the funeral service. He then told me that when he saw my mom's death announcement in the local newspaper, he was absolutely devastated and realized why she had not been able to attend his wife's services.

He said his wife just worshiped my mom and that she felt she could talk to her about everything and anything, that she truly was her best friend. He explained to me that mom's visits to their home were always marked on their kitchen calendar and his wife would always find a reason to have Anne come by, if for nothing else, just to talk and have coffee.

The woman with him, as it turned out, was his daughter, who was an aspiring model now living in Los Angeles. She told me that when she was a little girl, my mom would come to their home and give her little Avon samplers and sometimes would bring little surprises for her. She then told me that she was supposed to have gone back to Los Angeles the day before, but when she saw my mother's death announcement in the newspaper, she cancelled her trip. She said she wanted to come to the funeral home with her dad to pay her respects.

I was really touched by their story and the fond remembrance they had of my mother, the Avon Lady. More honestly, I was numbed by what they had shared with me. It totally blew me away!

As I said earlier, to my knowledge my mother never even had a business card with her name and title on it. But if she did, it might have read, "Anne Boughton, Avon Sales Representative and Prospective Best Friend." That's just who she was. As an Avon Lady she met and exceeded her objectives consistently. But, maybe more importantly, while she was working she touched the lives of others. She did her best to be a true friend to those she came in contact with.

I would guess my mother never knew that this gentleman's wife considered her to be her best friend. But if she had ever been made aware of this, I'm sure she would have been honored. Likewise, if my mother would have been given the choice between her quota achievements as an Avon sales representative or the personal relationships and friendships she made as a result of her Avon work, my guess would be that she would have chosen the latter. Most impressively, she was able to achieve success in both aspects of her work and life.

Our professional lives tend to have this absolutely amazing power, this attraction, this promise that consumes each and every one of us. In too many cases, it becomes our primary focus in life (even though we say it isn't) and we let it take over our lives. Much of this has to do with the fact that many of us have fooled ourselves and do believe we are what we do. Many of us define ourselves, establish our identities, based upon what we do for a living, the role that we play in the workplace. For many of us, this is how we seek our own sense of security in this world.

I recently attended a men's leadership seminar at my church and one of the questions asked of the group was, How many of you, when you die, would like to have your professional lives, including titles you have held and the companies you have worked for, chronicled on your tombstone? What a depressing thought. Needless to say, there were no takers in the room. We were then asked a different question and told to sit quietly and just think about how each of us would answer it individually. The question was: Who will be crying at your funeral?

I think we need to ask ourselves, "What is it that we *really* want from our professional lives?" Being part of a winning team? Feelings of self-worth through our accomplishments? Decent benefits that protect our family? An impressive title? A six-figure income? There are many ways to answer the question. However, with corporate mergers and acquisitions taking place on a daily basis, a global economy that can change overnight, technology advancing at an unbelievable pace and increasing competitive pressures in the marketplace, our business world is becoming more frantic, less stable and more unpredictable. Why would we ever believe that this is where we can find our security in today's world?

I go back to our story and I find myself asking what Billy's grandfather did in his professional life, in the workplace? Was he a laborer, a salesman, an engineer, an accountant, a teacher or college professor? Does it really matter? Do we really care? Whatever he did, he obviously learned some valuable lessons in his career along the way. We know this because what he shares with Billy about the missing piece pertains to bigger issues in life — issues about people and how we are all connected, about our responsibilities to one another and the importance of enjoying every moment that life has to offer.

No, we don't know what he did for a living. But, if we were to ask him for his input on the subject, I think he'd probably say something like, "Well, don't confuse making a living with making a life. Be thankful for every day in your life and live every day to the fullest. Oh, and when you go to bed at night, remind yourself, life is pretty darn good. Matter of fact, it might even be a little better come tomorrow."

Not bad advice.

Chapter 4

Financial Security, What Does It Really Buy?
What Is It Really Worth?

If you have never been to Mirror Lake in Lake Placid, New York, the setting of our story, it really is a very special place. It's nestled in a beautiful little valley amidst the Adirondack Mountains in upstate New York. Lake Placid is a mecca for Olympic history, having served as the host for the Winter Olympic Games in both 1932 and 1980. As one heads down Main Street, which is on the west side of Mirror Lake, there are a variety of quaint little shops and restaurants. Here you will find specialty stores, hotels, coffee shops, bookstores and souvenir shops, many of which are adorned with Olympic flags and flags from countries around the world. At the far end of Main Street, where its name actually changes to Mirror Lake Drive, is the beautiful Mirror Lake Inn. The Mirror Lake Inn was built in 1924 and with its dark, warm mahogany walls, polished walnut floors and stone fireplaces, it reeks of nostalgia, character and a very special coziness.

Past the inn on Mirror Lake Drive, the setting becomes more natural and rustic. The road begins to wind its way around the lake through a thicker, more dense, wooded area made up of pine trees, birch trees, elms and maples. Tucked in and out of this more wooded area are little meandering driveways that find their way back through the trees to some very nice homes and, in some cases, humble little cottages similar to the one Billy's grandfather lived in. It is, indeed, a beautiful place to be any time of day, regardless of the weather, regardless of the season. The lake sparkles, the leaves whisper their own sweet melody as the breezes dance through the trees and the clear, crisp fresh air is absolutely heavenly. There is no way you can buy this kind of natural beauty, this atmosphere, this kind of simplicity that obviously was what Billy's grandfather loved so much about Mirror Lake. No, money couldn't buy what he had found here. It truly is a little piece of heaven on earth.

For generations, many people have blamed the ills of the world on money. As the cliché goes, Money is the root of all evil. This is hardly the case, for in reality, it is one's obsession with money that typically brings out the worst in an individual. Money, by itself, is not evil at all. It merely is a medium of exchange that we use to equate value as we acquire goods or services in our society. It is what we use to complete our business transactions.

Many of us go through life trying to make as much money as we can. Some of this money we earn through our hard work, while some of it may come to us rather gratuitously through investments we might make, letting our money work for us. We do this so we can buy things, feed our families, accumulate stuff, take vacations, furnish our homes, send our kids to college, have nice retirements, etc. Hopefully, when we die, we have enough left over to pay off any remaining debts, pay for our own funeral and, maybe, have some left for the kids to fight over. That way, they can buy things, accumulate stuff, take vacations, buy their home, send their kids to college…you get the idea.

Money, when responsibly handled, can bring a certain degree of comfort and what many people feel is *real* security. Financial wealth becomes their definition of security. This is why many of us become so consumed with our professional lives. However, if financial security is the goal, when is enough, enough? I heard Ross Perot speak in 1998 and he said that our country was in a precarious situation because when people have times of great prosperity, which had been the case in the late '90s, and have too much money, they become "fat, dumb and complacent." Notice, he did not say fat, dumb and *happy*. Maybe we need to ask ourselves the question, "If money cannot buy happiness, what does financial security really buy us?"

Andrew Carnegie, the famous industrialist and philanthropist once said, "People work for money. If you want loyalty, buy a dog." This is an interesting statement because Andrew Carnegie was not making this statement about a bunch of Generation X'ers who were trying to become instant millionaires by launching their own dot-com company. Instead, he made this statement in an era when people in our country were more cognizant of certain values, values like loyalty, trust and the value of hard work.

Writing about this subject is somewhat difficult for me, almost a bit foreign. I say this because of the environment I was brought up in. Where I grew up, very little emphasis was put on money, or should I say, the accumulation of wealth. I did not have a single mentor who ever talked about the accumulation of money or financial security as a measure of or guarantee of success. My father did not, my mother did not, my coaches in youth sports, high school and college did not. My teachers from elementary school up through high school and college did not. The ministers that preached at our church did not. Bottom line: When I was growing up, none of the people who were a part of my life ever stressed to me that financial wealth had anything to do with one's success.

I grew up in an environment where there were a lot of middle-class, hard-working people. Many of the adults that I came in contact with — neighbors, parents of my friends, my mentors — had fought in World War II in the '40s. They were glad to be alive, and they were very happy to be Americans, building their lives and watching their families grow in a prosperous America. They never talked about financial security, nor were they obsessed with money. But there was one thing they were obsessed with: values; and their actions and the words they spoke made it clear what they believed in.

They were caring, hard-working, honest people and they were never too busy to lend a hand and help their neighbor. These were people that believed a man's word was as good as his handshake. From their example I learned that it was far more important to be honest than rich, because no man can ever buy his integrity, he can only earn it. They talked about the importance of loyalty. They talked about responsibility and expectations, what was expected of us and why it was important to push yourself in order to meet those expectations. They talked about the importance of working hard and trying to improve every day, not just once in a while. They talked about the value of competition, about winning, the pursuit of excellence and about achieving worthy goals. But, they never emphasized financial security or the accumulation of wealth as part of what mattered. Was this wrong?

It is important that we acknowledge the fact that money does play an important role in allowing us to make choices, to consider alternatives, and, in turn, be somewhat independent. Clearly, it is money that enables us to achieve the lifestyle that we want for our loved ones and ourselves. But, in reality, what does it really buy us in the long term? What guarantees does it give us?

Although we cannot buy the security we wish to have in our lives at any price, we continue to fool ourselves and tease ourselves endlessly with this notion that money and the accumulation of wealth is, in many ways, the key to our happiness and success.

In my past, I had often given this point serious thought. This typically would occur on a Sunday afternoon as I stood by my screened-in swimming pool, grilling steaks on my gas grill with an ice-cold beer in my hand. There, by myself, I would often think back to my childhood days and remember my dad grilling burgers on his cheap, little, hibachi grill which would be positioned on the corner of a two-step, concrete slab of cement that extended off the back of our house. In the Boughton household, this was affectionately referred to as the back porch.

I can see him now. He'd have on a pair of khaki Bermuda shorts and an old golf shirt with the collar stretched and worn. His dark black wavy hair combed straight back, his face and arms tanned from mornings and afternoons spent on the golf course. He was a handsome man. Armed with a spatula in one hand and one of his frothy whiskey sours in the other, he stood watch over that grill and enjoyed every second of it. There he was, the proud owner of a two-story, one and a half bath, colonial house situated in a very middle-class neighborhood, with a loving wife and three sons. He was as happy as a lark. I can honestly say that when I remember my dad standing by the grill in our backyard, he was always smiling. He was happy with his life. He was in love with his life.

Now, by comparison, my home was light years beyond what my dad had ever had. But, where was the smile on my face as I stood by the grill? Was I as happy as my dad had been? I had a loving wife and two sons and much to be thankful for. But, I also often found myself preoccupied with thoughts of my responsibilities on the job. There were proposals to be completed, sales calls to make and maybe a new presentation I was trying to develop. And of course, what about my financial matters, were they in order? What bills were coming due? Would my commissions be what I thought they were going to be? Here I was making a six-figure income, living in a beautiful Florida home, yet I was so concerned over my own financial security and everything associated with it, I couldn't even enjoy the moment, at least not like I wanted to. By comparison, my dad with his comparable paltry income and meager lifestyle was clearly the one with the bigger smile on his face. Why was I not as happy in my world as he was in his?

Some of it, I am sure, ties back to his life experiences, his perspective. His life, his puzzle, included some hardships that I cannot even begin to relate to. He was born in 1916 and he learned early on in his life about the hardship and devastation of World War I. His father (my grandfather) had been gassed in the war and while he survived, it left him with severely trembling hands. I still remember as a little boy watching him pick up a glass of iced tea to put it to his lips. To this day, whenever I hear ice cubes rattling in a glass, I think of him. As a teenager, my dad lived through the Great Depression and he saw people out of work, standing in bread lines. Then, in 1943, he went off to fight in World War II and while it was probably the greatest adventure of his life, it was probably also his worst nightmare. His mother died of a heart attack while he was in the service. He never spoke about it, but I often wondered if he felt his going off to war as her only child, might have been part of the reason for her death at such a young age. For him, like anyone who goes off to war, it changes one's life forever. Clearly, for everything he had seen in his life, for everything he had endured, his perspective on life was quite different from mine. After all, what hardships have I had to endure in my lifetime? What obstacles have I had to face?

Now, when I think about who my dad *really* was and what he had seen in his lifetime, I see him in a totally different light. Now, I understand that when he stood by the back porch grilling those burgers, drinking his whiskey sour on a Sunday afternoon, based upon everything he had seen in his lifetime, he probably thought, I'm the luckiest guy on the face of the earth. What a wonderful feeling to have. Somehow, he had found his own sense of security and was at peace with himself.

Today, the financial dynamics of our world economy are totally different. Interestingly, our children are also growing up with a totally different perspective about financial matters than many of us did. The changes that have occurred in our society in regard to money, the accumulation of wealth and our lifestyles will affect the way our children see their world in their lifetime.

For example, when I was a kid watching Mickey Mantle hit home runs for the New York Yankees, I thought he was the greatest baseball player in the world. I didn't think — Wow, is he going to be rich when he negotiates his next contract! It wasn't about money; it was about achievement, about breaking records, the real riches that could potentially stand the test of time. These things were far more important than money.

Today, there is a much different message out there for our children. Tiger Woods gets a 60-million-dollar deal to endorse Nike products. Michael Jordan makes incredible amounts of money endorsing everything from long-distance billing plans to Gatorade, and everybody reads about it, knows it, and potentially, aspires to it. The dot-com companies were all the rage on Wall Street as the New Millennium came into being, and individuals in their early twenties became multi-millionaires overnight when they took their companies public. Interestingly, less than one year later, many of these dot-com start-ups, once so highly touted, were either failing miserably or had already shut down, leaving many investors licking their wounds. Maybe Woody Hayes knew something about these companies and their failed business models long before their time when he uttered the words, "Anything that comes easy in life probably isn't worth a damn." Maybe he should have been a stock analyst instead of a head football coach.

No, financial security, the accumulation of wealth, offers us no guarantees. When it comes to our well-being, to something that *really* matters, maybe it's best to remember the words of Ralph Waldo Emerson, "The first wealth is health." What could be more true? When you lose your health, you lose everything.

There may be one other measure of wealth that does allow us to find some sense of security in this world. At my father's funeral in 1984, one of his friends made a very poignant comment to me about my dad. This guy, one of my little league baseball coaches who had coached alongside my dad for many years, looked at me and said, "Buddy, your dad was a rich man. Look at all these people who loved your father enough to come and pay their final respects to him here today." At that time in my life, being only thirty-three years old and very much focused on my career pursuits and making money, his comment hit a chord with me. Never in my life had I equated someone being rich based upon the personal relationships made in the course of their lifetime.

He was right. My father was a rich man, and he had lived a rich life. His friends from every walk of life were there that day. They came from his company, the church where he had been a founding member, the hospital where he had done volunteer work and the stroke club he and my mother had founded. In addition, teachers and coaches from the high school my brothers and I had attended plus men my father had coached in youth sports, came to pay their respects as well. It was an incredible show of love and affection. My dad's friend was right. Measured by the lives he touched, the friendships he had made and the relationships he had developed over the course of his life, my dad was a rich man. This was something that no stock options or IPO could ever have bought.

I think my dad and Billy's grandfather would have been great friends with one another. I think that because they were both people who, deep down, genuinely loved people for who they were — period. They really didn't care what you did for a living, how much money you made, how big a mortgage you had or what neighborhood you lived in. Instead, they cared about you, the person. They both loved people and life, and one thing is for sure, they each had a special affection for their grandchildren. Yup, they would have gotten along pretty well.

Oh, and as for the money thing? Well, they'd have agreed on that subject, too. They both knew how to squeeze a nickel.

Chapter 5

૭

Searching for Our Security through Relationships

I wonder if Billy's grandfather had many friends at Mirror Lake. My guess would be, probably not, at least not really close friends. After all, he was a guy. He probably had some good acquaintances, you know, people he knew in town and people who knew him. Maybe the closest thing he had to real friends were his buddies he would meet once a week on Tuesday mornings at the coffee shop on Main Street. Billy's grandfather was a likeable enough kind of guy, but he probably just didn't take the time to make friends and develop closer personal relationships.

We do know that he loved where he lived and I'm sure he valued being independent at his age, having his own place and his own space. My guess would be he read a lot, probably had his music playing in the background and, in the final assessment, might even have been a bit of an introvert. While I am sure he had his lonely moments, he also probably appreciated his solitude, understanding the difference between the two. If anything, maybe this was one thing he was lacking at this point in his life, some close personal relationships.

Our friendships, the personal relationships we establish over the course of our lives, play an enormous role in who we are as individuals and how we feel about ourselves. The people in our lives and the experiences we share with them largely contribute to how we see ourselves and the world we live in. In fact, maybe more than any other single facet of our lives, it may be through our personal relationships that we come the closest to finding any real sense of security in this world.

Just as every person is unique, so is every friendship and personal relationship we make. For example, we all have what I would call acquaintances, and then there are certain acquaintances who, in a time of need, truly become friends to us. How does one differentiate between the two? Well, I'm not exactly sure I can answer that. Although, I believe that most of us would think of our friends as those people we see on a more consistent basis and communicate with more frequently. I have heard said that one truly finds only five or six *real* friends in a lifetime. If that is the case, I believe that those friends, if indeed we are fortunate enough to have five or six such people in our lives, feel we can share our deepest feelings and maybe even our darkest secrets. These are not just friends but what I would call our most *intimate* friends.

Most of us guys are experts at having what I have referred to above as acquaintances. That's about all we need, or so we think. More realistically, it's about all we have time for. No, make that, it's all we *make* time for. Acquaintances are very low maintenance and typically both parties have very low expectations, if any at all, of one another. This makes these relationships very easy. With acquaintances there's always a friendly smile and an exchange of greetings, but it is a totally non-committal relationship. That's probably why it works so well for us guys. You never have a problem with someone who is merely an acquaintance.

However, true friendships, friendships that take us to a deeper level with another person, take time and effort. This is something that most men are not really excited about investing in. Let's face it, men are much more task-oriented than relationship-oriented and we stay busy by focusing on those tasks. For the most part, acquaintances tend to suit us just fine until, "it" happens.

"It" can be any number of things. You have a trauma in your life. A parent dies suddenly, you get fired from your job, your wife looks you in the eye and says she no longer loves you and wants a divorce. These are the times when you realize you wish you had more than just acquaintances. You wish you had a meaningful relationship with another human being, a relationship that truly mattered. That's when you wish you had a real friend.

It's natural to want this. None of us, men and women alike, want to live our lives in isolation, as an island. However, in order for this kind of relationship to exist — a relationship based on trust, honesty and a genuine caring for the other individual — it requires time, work and special effort on the part of both people. Again, this is why most men live their lives filled with acquaintances.

On the other hand, women do much better at developing these deeper, more intimate relationships. They should. Women tend to be more relationship-oriented and seek deeper, more meaningful relationships with their friends. Women are more open to honestly sharing their true feelings with one another once a certain level of trust has been established. They will discuss their concerns and their innermost thoughts with this other person with the confidence that their friend is there to listen without judging them. They have no fear of reprisal because for women, it has always been okay to show their emotions. Because of that, women can share with one another on an emotional level much better than men can. Men unfortunately, rarely, if ever, get there.

However, this is understandable. After all, most of us men got the same message when we were growing up: Big boys don't cry, right? This has long been the standard line offered up to any young boy starting probably at the age of four or five when he would be reduced to tears for whatever reason. We got a message early in our lives that to show emotion, especially something that brought tears to our eyes was, if anything, a sign of weakness. The message was clear: If you cry, you are weak. Many men, most unfortunately, have never let go of that mantra. They still live by it.

I will never forget the first time I ever saw a bunch of guys crying openly and unashamedly in the presence of one another. No, we weren't sitting in a circle beating drums out in the middle of some wooded area. Ironically, it happened while watching a movie that was about, of all things, a very special friendship between two men. What gave the story such gravity was that it was a true story about two professional football players. The date was November 30, 1971, and 48 million American homes along with the television in the lobby of my college dormitory were tuned in to what was then the most successful made-for-television movie in history, *Brian's Song*.

The movie was based on the true story of a friendship between Brian Piccolo and Hall of Fame running back, Gale Sayers, both of whom played for the Chicago Bears. Brian Piccolo was a persistent force in Gale Sayers' life after Sayers had experienced a career-threatening knee injury. Piccolo pushed Sayers and was instrumental in a successful rehabilitation effort that helped Sayers win the NFL's Most Courageous Player award for the 1969 season and establish himself as one of the all-time great running backs in the game. Unfortunately, Brian Piccolo's life took a different turn. He was diagnosed with a malignant tumor in one of his lungs.

Brian Piccolo and Gale Sayers were roommates on their road trips and with Piccolo being white and Sayers, black, this was an oddity in those times. Their friendship was, indeed, a very special friendship. But when Piccolo was diagnosed with the cancer and sent to New York for treatment, Sayers delivered a tribute in the locker room, in Brian's honor, to the rest of the Chicago Bears before one of their games. It is a very emotional scene and, of course, with the right music playing in the background, it really rips your guts out. I especially remember watching this scene and then looking around the room. Every guy, I mean each and every guy in the lobby that night, literally had tears streaming down his cheeks. Nobody said anything; there was total silence in the room. I will never forget that moment. Never before had I seen that sort of open display of emotion by young men, especially a bunch of college guys.

With no guarantees in life, it is probably all the more reason we need to let down our guard a little, admit to our true feelings and develop more meaningful personal relationships in our lives. Life is filled with wonderful moments and these are so much more enjoyable and memorable when shared with our friends, people we genuinely care about and people who genuinely care about us. Life is also very fragile and in a heartbeat, any one of us can be impacted by trauma, hardship or difficulties.

September 11th taught us a lesson about this, about how unpredictable and fragile life can be. It also taught a lot of us that it is okay to cry in public when we are so moved. Amidst the horror of that day it was not uncommon across America to see women and men alike with tears streaming down their faces. On our city streets, total strangers reached out to one another for comfort and we held each other and cried unashamedly. We all felt the pain; we all felt a sense of loss. As one of my friends said, "We all died just a little on that day."

All of us will suffer some personal traumas in our lives. It's part of life, part of the great mystery. We don't know why certain things happen, but they do, and when they do, we need our friends. It is in our darkest hours that we need the love and support of our friends the most. It is important to have friends to whom we can open our hearts and minds. We need each other.

As I have grown older and hopefully, a little wiser, I have made a choice to be more open about sharing my true feelings with many of my friends. For me, maybe it was going through my divorce, losing both of my parents, and watching my two sons grow up and leave home that helped me to open up more. Then again, maybe it was because I have reached a point in my life where I really don't care if people choose to judge me or think anything less of me because of how I feel or because I am willing to share my feelings more openly with them. As I have gotten older, I have learned that this quality, our ability to feel and genuinely care for one another, is truly what makes us human. It is the great differentiator that separates us from all of the other species that share this planet with us. So, when we fail to admit we have feelings, that we are untouched by other people and the events in our lives, we are, in effect, denying we are human.

Life is short and if we truly care about another person, then we need to let that person know just how much we do care about them. Otherwise, we may, through some twist of fate, never have the opportunity again to say what we wanted to say to that person. If we don't do this, we risk living a life filled with only acquaintances.

I think of a dear friend of mine who lost his father very suddenly when we were both relatively young men. We were in our late twenties and working for the same company. As guys go, we were very good friends and we continue to be today. Following his father's death, he had a very difficult time with the grieving process. Finally one night, he explained to me that he had never really told his father how much he loved him and how much he appreciated everything he had done for him. I wanted so much to do something for my friend, to fix his problem, but I couldn't. What was done could not be undone. My friend was not only grieving for the loss of his father, but also for words that had gone unsaid. There was nothing I could say, nothing I could do. I sometimes think of this today and wonder how many people on this planet have had that same regret. How many people have wanted to say something, something really special to a friend or loved one, but have just had too much trouble getting the words out?

I was fortunate. In the home where I grew up, telling my parents how much I loved them was an everyday occurrence. It just happened. Don't ask me why. We just hugged a lot in our family and when we did, we told each other we loved each other. Of course, for most of us guys, telling another person outside of your immediate family how much you really value their friendship, how much you care about them, is a difficult and awkward thing to do. Now, throw in the "love" word, and for most guys, we're talking impossible!

Isn't that weird? As guys go, we are pretty passionate about a lot of things in life and in describing such things, using the word "love" seems very natural. For example, I can think of a million different things that I might say I love in this life because, quite frankly, I am pretty passionate about life. For example, I love college football. I love ice hockey. I love college basketball's Final Four! I love watching the Masters every year from Augusta. I love the U.S. Open, the British Open and the Ryder Cup. I love the Indianapolis 500. I love pizza and Buffalo wings. I love going to the beach. I love Thanksgiving. I love New York City. I love sitting in a big-city bar at 2 A.M. and playing *New York State of Mind* by Billy Joel on the jukebox as waiters prepare to close for the night. I love coming home after a vacation and crawling into my own bed. I love the fall and watching the leaves change color. I love bitter cold winter nights when the snow squeaks under my shoes. I love the sound of the wind blowing, any time of year. I love an ice-cold beer on a hot summer afternoon, and I love the smell of freshly cut grass (where did that one come from?). Men will say they love a lot of things, but when it comes to other people, for a lot of men, that's a tough one. Why is that?

Even Budweiser made light of this (not meant to be a play on words) with its "I love you, man!" Bud Light commercials. Why is it that when it comes to the most important aspect of our lives, other people, some of us have such a difficult time saying "I love you" to our dearest friends, friends that we genuinely do love? Isn't it strange that so many of us men are so paralyzed by our own feelings and find it so awkward and difficult to admit or verbalize those feelings?

I have very meaningful, deep friendships with some guys. Some have been life-long friends. Several others are from high school, college, and a couple are from my professional life. In some cases, I knew their parents, their brothers and sisters and the houses they grew up in. Now that we are older, I also can say that I've watched their kids grow up and they have watched mine do the same. These are people who have been there for me in times of need, and I have tried to be there for them as well. When I see these guys, especially if we have not seen each other for months or in some cases, years, I embrace them in my arms and tell them how glad I am to see them. With these friends, a hand-shake isn't enough for me. God knows I genuinely care about these people; I do love them. However, there was a time in my life when I found it very difficult to look these friends of mine in the eye and tell them that I genuinely loved them. Why is that? Why should that be so difficult?

But that was the old me. Now, if I love someone and I genuinely care about them that much, I just come out and tell them so. I want them to know they are that special to me. If they think I'm weird for telling them that, for openly expressing my feelings, then that's their choice to feel that way, and it's okay with me. For whatever reasons, most men have totally misinterpreted this whole "emotions, I love you, feelings" thing. My opinion: We need to get over it, give up our macho man façades and get real — period.

Ah, but there is a catch, isn't there? Friendships are not automatic. We cannot make someone like us. We cannot force someone to be our friend. And yes, even the friendships we do make and the relationships we find ourselves involved in do not come with any guarantees. People are more transient today, and it is not uncommon to meet someone, establish a wonderful friendship with them, only to see them move away six months later. You say you'll stay in touch and you mean well, but after the first four weeks and several long-distance telephone calls, you and your friend get on with your lives without each other. It just happens.

Sometimes friendships we make are a by-product of some activity. For example, parents often come together and make new friends because of their children's involvement in youth sports or some other activity. But, after weeks of fund-raising efforts, the games and post-game parties, when the season ends, so do the friendships. Oh, we may bump into each other at the grocery store, but it is rare when we make the effort to extend those relationships.

Of course, the worst situation of all is when friendships end over harsh words or disagreements. It is unfortunate but not all that unusual to see two people bond to become the best of friends and then, for whatever reason, a disagreement, a difference of opinion, turn and go their separate ways. This is sad but a grim reality that many of us have experienced at one time or another in our life.

So, clearly, even our best friendships do not come with a guarantee. If this kind of relationship does not come with a guarantee, how can we ever expect to find our sense of security here?

As one gets older, we learn to value everything in life so much more with every passing day, including our personal relationships. Unfortunately, it is only with age that this kind of wisdom begins to come to us and bring us to this revelation, this reality. Billy's grandfather had this kind of wisdom.

As for the friends, the personal relationships that were part of Billy's grandfather's life, well, we can only guess as to what they might have been. I guess that he certainly had some friends, people he could count on and people who might, when needed, count on him. More than having friends though, Billy's grandfather understood how important it was to *be a good friend* to others. Oh, he definitely knew this. Otherwise, how would he ever have been able to articulate the story of the missing piece to his grandson?

Chapter 6

☙

Our Search for Security Through Marriage

We know that Billy's grandfather was married at one time. In fact, he was married for some forty-seven years, almost two-thirds of his life. Unfortunately, that marriage ended when Billy's grandmother was tragically killed. It was like any other gray, overcast November day at Mirror Lake. Cold, a light mist in the air, with darkness settling in late in the afternoon, she innocently stepped from the curb to cross the street. A tourist, unfamiliar with the traffic and pedestrian patterns down on Main Street, turned his vehicle right into her. He never even saw her. It was one of those unexplained tragedies we read about in the newspaper every day. For most of us, we turn the page and the event passes. For Billy's grandfather and their entire family, it would be something they would never forget.

We don't know how long ago that was. What we do know from our story is that Billy's grandfather appears to have gotten past this trauma in his life. Somehow, even though suffering a very painful loss, he was able to move on and regain his love for life. He still was able to see the good things life had to offer, even when he was dealing with this unforeseen tragedy.

This mindset, this belief that there is more good in life than bad, became part of who he is. Bad weather couldn't ruin his day with his grandson even though it forced them to change their plans. And when they had completed their puzzle, all but for one missing piece, he again was able to find good in the situation. So, perhaps, looking back on it now, while he might not ever find good in the fate that he had suffered in losing his wife so tragically, maybe, just maybe, he was able to find some meaning from it. Maybe there was something he could learn from the experience and in doing so, somehow, he could be a better person for the experience. There was indeed a certain resilience that Billy's grandfather possessed, a passion that let him not only survive, but live life to its fullest.

Was he always like that? Maybe. Or is it possible that the loss of his wife had actually enlightened him as to how very precious every single day of life really is? Once again, we may not know the answers to these questions, but one thing is for sure. While Billy's grandfather was now living alone, much of what was living inside of him — his spirit, his soul, his zest for life — was in part and in some way, shape or form, the result of his spending forty-seven years of his life with his loving and devoted wife. There is no denying that part of who Billy's grandfather had come to be in his lifetime was a result of the marriage relationship that he had experienced with his wife. That's part of the connection we have to each other, part of our puzzle; and in a marriage, that relationship can be, and many times is, the strongest of all our connections.

There is no denying that marriage is how many of us, both men and women, seek some sense of security in our lives. That is why it is a topic that must be included in this book. In fact, I would say that of all the topics that make up Part II of this book, marriage more than any other topic serves as the best example of how we as individuals consciously seek some form of security or acceptance in our lives. There is nothing that exemplifies this more in our adult lives than the fact that we make a sincere, and, I emphasize, a *conscious* effort, to find the right partner to spend the rest of our lives with. In doing so, we hope to find some sense of security.

Once again, in case you did not read the introduction at the front of the book, I feel the need for a disclaimer in writing this chapter. I am not a professional psychologist, marriage counselor or family therapist, so who am I to even try to address this topic? Maybe worse, according to my hockey buddies, I am a slow learner when it comes to the marriage thing. Yes, it's true, I did marry and go through divorces, twice, with the same woman. And, yes, I am at the time of this writing (and I would expect it to be no different in the future), very happily married to a beautiful, caring and loving woman who once was my elementary school sweetheart. At twelve years of age, she was the first girl I ever kissed. So, do I believe in the institution of marriage? Absolutely! Am I an expert on the subject? Certainly not, but I have learned some valuable lessons along the way, lessons that hopefully make me a better partner now, even a better person, than I was when I first got married.

Like it or not, the institution of marriage is a clear confirmation that very few of us really want to live out our lives alone. There is no doubt that life is far better, far richer, when shared with someone you truly love. But as in every other aspect of life, there are no guarantees in a marriage. I have learned this in my lifetime. So did Billy's grandfather.

I can relate a little bit to Billy's grandfather. He is living his life alone after being married for a number of years. I've been there. It isn't easy, especially if the loss of your spouse is unexpected, be it through a tragic accident or a divorce that you had no fore-warning of. Mine was the second variety, the one where you don't see it coming at all and then you turn around one night and get hit in the face with what feels like a Tiger Woods' 5-iron. That hurts.

Marriage can be a lot of things. It can be heavenly bliss, and it can be a living hell. It can be two people coming together as partners and best friends, caring for one another and always trying to help each other, or it can be two people competing against one another for success, for their own pleasures and for their own interests. It can be a loving relationship where each person demonstrates a willingness to let go and, if necessary, even sacrifice for the benefit of their partnership over their own individual interests. Or, it can be an ongoing struggle, one where each person cares more about *who* is right than *what* is right and comes to expect more from their partner than they themselves are willing to give.

We all know how difficult it is to make a marriage work in today's society. There are numerous stresses and influences that, if allowed to, can test any marriage. In addition to these stresses is the simple fact that the partners in a marriage, change over time making them in some ways different individuals than who they were when they exchanged their wedding vows.

As we have discussed, men and women are very different to begin with. Men are more task-oriented, women more relationship-oriented; men are not open to sharing their feelings (if they can get in touch with them to begin with), women look for emotional connections. So, it is no wonder that marriage relationships can be difficult. Why, then, do we enter our marriages thinking this may be where we are going to find some sense of security in our lives?

Statistics certainly confirm that there are no guarantees when we get married. When I went through my divorce, it was the most devastating thing I had ever experienced in my lifetime and I felt totally alone. The statistics didn't matter to me, I just never, ever thought I would go through a divorce. For me, I could not even imagine it; it was unconscionable.

I know now I was not alone in feeling that way. I have since talked with many men and women who had their spouse leave them and in many of those cases, while they admit that they did not have a perfect marriage (who does?), they never expected their partner in life to walk out on them. For me, not only was I hurt by it, but I also had trouble understanding it. How could this happen to me?

As the therapists would say, "We had the picture." My wife of more than sixteen years was a beautiful woman, and we had two happy, healthy boys. We had a lovely home in the suburbs. I made good money. We paid our bills on time, took nice vacations and enjoyed good health. Our boys were great kids. They did well in school. My wife and I were active in our church, PTA, and the boys' activities such as scouting and youth sports. I had always been fairly successful in my life (speaking of my pursuits academically, athletically, socially, professionally, etc.), and I felt pretty good about my life and who I was. I had no complaints. To that point, my life had gone quite well and certainly, more than anything else, nothing mattered more to me than my family. And yet, here I was at the age of thirty-eight facing the most painful and difficult dilemma of my life: my wife was leaving me and my family was breaking apart. I kept asking myself, How could this be happening to me? But, it did. Our marriage ended in divorce.

Why do marriages end in divorce? I guess there are a zillion different reasons. Just sit in a bar some evening and survey the divorced people who are there. The stories, the reasons they got divorced, are endless. It seems there is only one consistent, recurring thread when you listen to these testimonies: very rarely do you hear, "Well, it was my fault."

Maybe divorce is so prevalent in this country because as we are brought up, we are taught and educated about a lot of things in life but not on how to make our marriages work. So, is the answer a required course in high school, a "Marriage 101" if you will, that addresses everything from financial planning, budgeting, domestic care for the home, sex and the marriage relationship, respectful treatment of our spouses, proper parenting, conflict resolution, etc.? Is this the answer to our rising divorce rate and breakdown of the traditional family in the United States, formal education on the subject?

How did so many of our parents keep their marriages together? Most of our parents had no formal training on how to make their marriages work. In fact, they had less of an understanding than supposedly we do today when it comes to issues like nurturing intimacy in the relationship, communicating our true feelings and validating those of our marriage partner. C'mon, my dad, "validating feelings"? I don't think so! Maybe there is credence to the expression, "Ignorance is bliss?"

For our parents, maybe it is true that everyday life for them was simpler and the pressures less severe than what we live with today. Certainly, the roles of husband and wife, male and female, were more clearly defined at that time. Men were expected to work outside the home, slaying the dragons and making a living while the women stayed at home to nurture the young and take care of the domestic chores. In the '50s and early '60s, that was very much life in America.

Then again, maybe our parents were able to hold their marriages together in part because of what they had already seen and experienced in their lives. Coming out of World War II, they were survivors and just glad to be alive and to have what they had, living in America. So, maybe it was this perspective that helped them always see the glass as half-full instead of half-empty, not only in their marriages but in many aspects of their life. Regardless, some how, some way, they managed to keep their marriages and their families together.

When I hear today of a couple that is going through a divorce, it saddens me. I can remember my own pain from both of my divorces (yes, from the same woman) and I remember what it felt like to lose my identity as husband, father-at-home, protector and provider. Divorce is never easy, and often it gets ugly and complicated. Even worse, it often involves children. At a time when I would have done absolutely anything to protect my two sons from someone else hurting them, ironically, it was their parents who would end up hurting them the most. I still struggle sometimes when I think about that aspect of our divorce: the trauma that it caused for our two sons at such a young age in their lives.

Several months after our divorce was finalized, for the first and only time in my career, I was asked for my resignation, citing my inability to stay focused on my work. Now, I had lost my wife, my home, the daily presence of my two sons in my life, and just for good measure, my job. More than ever, I realized it was my marriage that had served as the foundation for my security in life. When it failed, my world crumbled around me and I found myself dealing with what was the most painful thing, emotionally, I had ever encountered.

And yet, for all the pain, the suffering, the feelings of devastation that so many of us have experienced and endured as a result of our marriages failing, we find ourselves seeking a sense of belonging, of acceptance, of security through, of all things, another marital relationship. Why are we so convinced that the second time, or third time, or fourth time, we will *find* the right partner, the right chemistry, and the magic that will make the next marriage different?

Maybe it goes back to an expectation that says, this time, I am not going to make the same mistake. Well, it stands to reason; we should be smarter the second time around, right? But time and time again, I hear how someone defines their own "being smarter" by saying that this time they are going to find "the right partner." The right partner? Is there such a thing, and if there really is, what are our chances of finding them in this world? Really, think about that. What are the odds of finding that one very special person somewhere in this world that could be defined as the right partner?

I really don't believe that marriage is meant to be like a scavenger hunt. I don't think that finding the supposed right partner is what determines the fate or destiny of a marital relationship. In terms of your marriage partner, what is there in the beginning — well, that's all there is! It's kind of a "what you see, is what you get" thing and, believe me, everyone has their warts, even if some of us disguise them better than others do. But, that is merely the starting point. What we create going forward in our marriages is what we *choose* to create.

In order to create something of value in our marriages, we must be willing to invest in the relationship. For the most part, keeping a marriage together is about growing in the relationship. This typically involves accepting change, making good choices and staying committed to your partner. Well, if that doesn't spell out the root of the problem, what does? How many of us can honestly say we do well with change, always make good choices and are willing to commit ourselves totally to another individual for life? Hello?

Growth in a marital relationship also takes time and this requires some patience. Patience? Hmmm, there's another virtue we are all just filled with today, right? But the truth is, nothing of any real value is *created* in an instant, other than maybe a memory that may last for a lifetime. If we are talking about creating something that takes conscious effort and will have true, lasting value, it is not going to happen overnight. This is a fundamental law of nature and this is true in marriage. When we think we can do otherwise and violate or circumnavigate this basic law of nature, that some things take time, we are kidding ourselves. That is when we show how fundamentally flawed we are as human beings. Unfortunately, we all too often think and act as though we are the ones in control and attempt to supercede or violate the laws of nature.

As Billy's grandfather said, he learned from the seasons. The *changes* that Mother Nature brings to our world with every season, these wondrous miracles of change, are something we can learn from. For one, they occur in their own time. No one can demand when the leaves change colors in the fall nor can one command the flowers to bloom earlier in the spring. These miracles take place according to Mother Nature's time schedule. Also, we need to appreciate the diversity of the seasons and welcome the changes as they occur. Maybe too, then, we should expect certain changes in our marital relationships. Nothing ever stays the same. If nothing ever stays the same, why should our relationship with our spouse? People grow, people change, and with those changes comes the need to accept, even welcome, change. For many of us, this is much easier said than done.

The commitment that two people bring to the marital relationship, however, that is what needs to be steadfast and rock-solid if the marriage is to be everlasting. That cannot change. It is the commitment that must be honored and held to as steadfast if there is to be any sense of security that is to come from a marital relationship.

Billy's grandfather and grandmother understood this. They had married each other when they were in their early twenties and despite the hardships, the changes, the things they did not like about each other, they honored their commitment to one another. They knew that given the choice, they would rather work together, stay together, and create their own little piece of heaven with each other on this earth than to come to know the hell of being alone.

Unfortunately, Billy's grandfather had no choice in the matter. As much as he loved his wife, fate would cast a dark shadow over his life on a cold, November day and he would learn what it is like to live alone. Maybe that is why he is such a good grandfather and such a special person to his grandson.

Now, more than ever, he knows just how important every person in his life, every piece in his puzzle, really is. Like every day of his life, he cherishes each and every piece in his puzzle.

Chapter 7

Searching for Security through Parenthood

We know from our story what Billy's grandfather was like as a grandfather, but I wonder what he was like as a father to his own son. As a grandfather, he was wonderful. He was caring, warm, loving and seemed to be a very genuine kind of man. He had that special kind of wisdom and perspective that most older people, like our grandparents, seem to have. He was a patient man, at least he was with his grandson, and he never seemed to be in much of a hurry. Maybe that was one of the lessons he had learned from the changing seasons. He also knew how to make life enjoyable. He was fun to be around, at least his grandson thought he was. Papa definitely had a sense of humor and to go with it, an attitude that was characterized by both resilience and spontaneity. These traits were probably due to the fact that in his own way, Billy's grandfather was a pretty creative individual. All things considered, he was a role model who knew how to both love and inspire in a fatherly way. But, I wonder what he was like as a father to his own son?

One thing I will say based upon my own experience is this: Being a parent is not easy. In fact, being responsible for the safe and proper upbringing of a child that you bring into this world, may create more feelings of inadequacy and insecurity than anything else that I know of. At the same time, it can be the most enriching, wonderful experience in one's entire life. Regardless how one views the opportunity of being a parent and the responsibility that goes with it, raising kids in today's world can be a real crapshoot. As I have said on every topic we have touched on so far in Part II, there are no guarantees. Nothing could be truer when it comes to our children.

Of course, I am a guy and that is my perspective. On the other hand, I have had many women tell me that they have a much different perspective when it comes to the issue of parenting. There are many women who have dreamed of and looked forward to the day that they would, in fact, become a mother. These women have dreamed of this moment much of their life and now, the child that was growing inside them comes into this world as another human being. This experience, becoming a mother, is a *defining moment* in a woman's life. For many men, while it is a significant event to become a father, it still does not take on quite the same meaning as it does for a woman. Quite frankly, how could it? When one considers what women go through in bearing a child, compared to what men have to do, well, excuse me guys, it clearly is more of a defining moment for a woman than it is for a man. I think, however, that the older a man is when he becomes a father, the more he has already seen of the world and experienced in his own life, the more significance comes with the realization that he is now a father. It is rare for young men (late teens, early twenties) who become fathers at such an early age in their adulthood to appreciate the magnitude of what they have done and the responsibility they now need to bear. Of course, I make this statement based upon my own experience.

Nevertheless, to be part of a loving relationship with another human being and through that love, consummate life and watch that life come into the world is an absolutely incredible experience. To see that child emerge from the mother's womb and take its first breath of life is to truly witness a miracle. I will never forget watching my wife give birth to our older son on what was a cold December day in 1975. I grew up a lot that day.

I remember taking my wife into the hospital and watching a nurse wheel her down the hall in a wheelchair to a labor room. She was only twenty-two at the time and as I stood in the hallway watching them continue their way down the hall, I thought how afraid she must be and realized how helpless I was. For her, there would be no turning back. No matter what her fears or how much pain she would go through, she was going to give birth to our child. Life suddenly took on a totally different perspective for me.

But, without question, be it for a man or woman, bringing a new life, a child, into the world can be both a blessing and at the same time a frightening, intimidating experience. In some respects, becoming a parent can lead to tremendous feelings of anxiety, insecurity and vulnerability. Why do I say this?

The world can be a very scary place. It was in many respects in the mid- to late '70s when my children were born, and it certainly is today. While we struggle to find or create some sense of security for ourselves as adults, creating and trying to guarantee that security for our children is even more difficult and frightening. In fact it is impossible. All one has to do is read the newspaper on any given day.

While death is a common denominator for us all, the age at which we die is not. I knew one family in the community where I grew up where the parents lost all three of their children to untimely deaths. I often wondered, how did those parents continue on in life after losing not one, not two, but all three of their children before they themselves died? This hits directly at the paradoxical nature of having children. While being a parent can certainly be one of the most rewarding, fulfilling experiences we can experience, it can also be one of the most frustrating and stressful experiences one ever encounters in life.

I have countless memories with each of my sons — some good, some not so good, and some that are really very special to me. When I think of those very special memories, I can almost go back and relive those moments. It's as though my senses come alive and I transcend back to that very moment in time. I can smell the smells all over again, I hear the sounds and I even feel the air temperature. Whether it's watching my older son experience the thrill of sledding down a snow-covered hill for the first time in his life or running alongside my younger son as he learned to ride a bicycle, those moments are as real for me today as when they occurred in my life. They were magical moments in my life, and best of all, no one can ever take them away from me. So, do I believe that bringing a child into this world changes who you are as an individual? Absolutely! It most definitely gives you a different perspective of life and the world we live in. Life is never the same after you bring a child into this world.

As I examine my experiences as a parent, I think of three distinct things I have learned or, am still in the process of learning.

For one, I have found and am still learning that the hardest thing to do as a parent is to not do *everything* for your children.

This was a difficult concept for me to grasp as a very young twenty-four year-old first-time father, and I have continued to wrestle with it ever since. When do I (should I) let them go on their own, making their own decisions, knowing full well that they may experience failure, fall down, and have to deal with the consequences? This is a very difficult thing to do, but it is something we must learn to do as parents. It is part of the *letting go* that all parents struggle with but must learn. To let go of our children is part of our responsibility as parents.

Failure and pain are both part of life. If life was always wonderful, a perfect world, a utopia, would we, could we, ever really experience joy? Hardship and pain are often the cornerstones of character. As much as we want to protect our children, we must remind ourselves that someday we will not be here for them. There are no guarantees with our children. They are our legacy in name only. In time, they will make a life of their own and make their own choices, with or without our approval. Our job is not to keep them dependent upon us but instead to teach them to be independent and lead productive, responsible lives on their own. As difficult as it may be to *let go* of our children, that is part of our responsibility as parents.

Second, I have learned that there is a big difference between *loving* our children and *accepting* our children. Being able to do both can be challenging for even the most open-minded of parents. This issue of loving and accepting is one that becomes more of a challenge as a child gets older and enters adolescence. Let's face it, when the kids are young, it is much easier to be in absolute control as a parent. We buy their clothes for them, and then we tell them what they are going to wear, along with how they will wear their hair, etc. It's pretty straightforward. When a child gets older, however, being accepted by their peers becomes more important to them. This is just a natural part of their socialization. As part of this process, children begin to establish their own identities as individuals. Unfortunately, the new identity is often something that a parent cannot or does not want to accept, and conflict arises. Now, in some cases where a child exhibits certain behaviors or practices, be they illegal or potentially causing harm to themself or to others, the behavior should absolutely not be accepted or tolerated. But, I am not talking about those kinds of extremes. It is the lesser ones where we seem to come into our most challenging conflicts.

Unfortunately, as parents, we are often quick to judge our children. All too many times, we forget who they are and how much we really do love them. As Mother Teresa once said, "If all you do is judge people, you will never have time to love them." There is nobody in this world for whom I have unconditional love more for than my two sons, but oh, how I have often struggled accepting some of their decisions and the choices they made. Fortunately, I have a loving wife, their stepmother, who counsels me on this subject and helps me realize that while they are still my children and always will be, they also are adults who are entitled to lead their own lives.

However, this issue — the loving versus accepting of our children — is a tough one for many parents and sadly it is this very issue that often leads to painful separations between a parent and a child. Sometimes it is our love for them, our parenting nature, that makes the accepting so difficult.

My third and final point is clearly the most important. Our children complete us. What I mean by that is that we learn things through our relationships with our children that we might otherwise have never learned. There was an example of this in our story when Billy's grandfather realized, after the fact, that he had never before thought of how our lives are like puzzles until he related it to his grandson that day. Even at times when we might not have wanted to learn something, to change, it is our children who sometimes force us to learn and ultimately change.

When you raise children, you no longer have certain choices or options. You are forced to deal with issues and doing so forces you to grow and to learn in the process. The choices are taken away. There are no options.

Maybe one of the most difficult things we are forced to learn is that no matter how good a job we try to do raising our children — loving them, supporting them in their endeavors, disciplining them as needed — when it comes to the ultimate fate of our children, we are never really in control. No matter how much we try to do as parents, in the end, there will come a time when our children have to make their own choices. If they make the wrong choice, and act on it, the consequences that follow may be dire.

This became a painful and startling reality for our family in 1992. A young girl who was a close friend of our older son was killed in a car accident on the way to the beach during spring break. This young lady, then a sophomore in high school, had been my older son's first elementary school crush. We had gotten to know her in her elementary school years as just a child, another second grader in Brad's class. She was a darling girl with a wonderful personality and a cute smile. She and my son had remained close and were good friends through middle school and into high school. But now she was gone.

Bringing a child into the world as a parent is a natural process, it has order to it, and it is the norm. But for a parent to lose a child, this is not the norm. I struggled with this. How does any parent cope as we watch a child, a child that could have just as easily been your own, leave this world? It is bad enough to lose a child due to disease or illness but so much worse, to lose a child so suddenly through some tragic, traumatic twist of fate. Nothing could be more painful. Nothing could be more unnatural. As a parent, where does one find a security in times like that?

These are those rare moments, the wake-up calls, which shake us out of our monotonous, everyday way of life and bring us back to reality. So many times as parents we fight the wrong battles with our kids for the wrong reasons. I remember going through a battle with my older son when he was sixteen. He wanted to get his ear pierced. He was playing high school lacrosse at the time and almost every kid on the team had his ear pierced. This was a constant sore spot between my son and me. Finally, I gave in and he got his ear pierced, much to my dismay. This all took place about two weeks before the car accident that took the young girl's life during spring break.

I will always remember going to her memorial service. The church was absolutely packed to capacity. In attendance were relatives, friends of her family, parents of many of her friends and of course, many, many of her high school friends. To see all of those young kids, kids that I knew, great looking kids with bright futures, and to know that now, she was gone forever, was very emotional. I remained composed but when I got to my car in the parking lot, I just lost it. I just stood there sobbing as I leaned against my car. As my wife came to comfort me, she gently put her arm around me and whispered in my ear, "That pierced ear isn't such a big deal now, is it?" She was so right.

I remember once asking a man whom I have tremendous respect for and who is my senior by some fifteen or twenty years, how he had raised his children to be so successful. One had graduated from Brown, the other from Princeton, both were quality individuals and had done quite well in their personal and professional lives. At the time, my boys, Brad and Cory, were nineteen and fifteen, and I was in a bit of a struggle with them both since they weren't following the path I thought they should.

I remember him laughing at my question and saying, "Oh, what you don't know!" He went on to tell me some pretty eye-opening stories about his son during his college years. But, he then put a hand on my shoulder and gave me this advice. He said to me, "All children choose a path of their own and all you can do is be there to pick them up and dust them off when they do fall down. In reality, a parent's only job is to keep 'em alive from the time they're twelve 'til they're about twenty-five. You give 'em the right foundation, the right values, just keep 'em alive, and you'll be surprised. They come around about the time they're twenty-four or twenty-five. That's all you can do."

I have always found comfort in that advice. Some people may not agree with it, but I think there is a lot of truth in it. Quite honestly, I think it sounds like something Billy's grandfather would have said. Maybe that's why I like it.

Chapter 8

☙

Searching for Security through
Our Individual Activities

I wonder what kind of stuff Billy's grandfather did when he was a younger man? I'm not sure we will ever know, but we did have a few clues in our story. We know he liked music, so maybe he played a musical instrument in his younger years. We know he liked the outdoors, and he lived on beautiful Mirror Lake in the midst of the Adirondack Mountains in upstate New York. Maybe he did a lot of camping, fishing and hiking. Come to think of it, he seemed to know a lot about Mount Rainier. Maybe he'd been there in his youth and had hiked in the Cascades or climbed some of the mountains in that region. Whatever he had done in terms of his activities and his personal interests, did it really matter? Did it matter to his grandson?

One cannot, however, overlook Papa's private thoughts near the end of the story. As he stood at his kitchen sink looking out onto Mirror Lake, he looked back on his life, the people in it and some of the things he had and had not done. Had he lived a full life or could he, should he, have done more with his life? Was he satisfied with the life he had lived and the person he had come to be?

This may be a question that each of us asks of ourselves as we get older and head into the autumn of our lives. Yet, it could be a question we ask ourselves at the end of every day. Did I really *live* today? Did I really do all I could have and should have done to make this day everything it had the potential to be? Sounds kind of like *carpe diem* on steroids. However, as adults in *today's world,* how do we truly *live* every day to the fullest? Is it really that easy, just making a conscious choice to make each day all that it can be?

Unfortunately, our lives have become cluttered; cluttered with information overload, media hype, noise, new technology and just the general stuff that we all seem to fill up our lives with. We seem to be running around at a frantic, hectic pace. Why is it that so many of us are so busy all the time?

Between our professional responsibilities, the personal obligations we have to our spouses and children and just the everyday responsibilities that come with owning a home, taking care of the many odds and ends that come up, how can we do it all and do for ourselves, too? This begs the question: Why is it important to take time for ourselves?

Obviously, we need to take time to reflect, to contemplate and just think. It is important to relax, recharge our batteries and replenish our brain cells, our spirit and our souls. It's just as important to take time to rejuvenate ourselves physically and get regular exercise. This may be best accomplished by exploring some of our personal interests that involve physical activity and actually making the effort to experience, firsthand, some of those activities. In many respects, it is through a combination of our own introspection and our physical exploits that we enrich our lives and define *who* we are as individuals.

Whether we realize it or not, many of us seek to find our sense of security not through our relationships or our professional endeavors, but by what we choose to do in the way of individual activities. All too often, however, many of us have ideas, dreams, deep down inside us about what it is that we would really like to do, and yet, we never act on those ideas. Unfortunately, too many times, we let our dreams die.

Disagree? Then, someone, please help me understand why there are so many people today in their late thirties up through their early fifties going through a so-called mid-life crisis? They live in comfortable homes, lead productive lives and are responsible, law-abiding, tax-paying citizens. They are enjoying good health, living a nice lifestyle in a country that has the highest standard of living in the world, raising a family, what could be missing? Why all the frustration and unhappiness? Why all the feelings of emptiness?

In many cases, it is our conflicting, almost overwhelming responsibilities (many of which are self-imposed) that leave us with a lack of free time that, in turn, keeps us from pursuing some of the individual activities that we would like to experience in our lives. This often leads many of us to what can be a very painful and introspective thought process when we choose to ponder the possibilities of both our past and future: If only I had taken the time, made the time, prioritized differently, I could have filled what is this gaping "black hole" in my life with meaningful, incredible human experiences — experiences that would have made a difference in my life. Experiences that could have, maybe would have, made me a different, better, more complete person than who I am today.

Some of this is changing. Today, more than ever, Americans are starting to venture out. They suddenly want more out of life and quality of life issues are becoming more of a priority to people. As a result, people are trying new things. They are taking white-water rafting trips, painting lessons, practicing yoga, going on adventure vacations, running marathons, skydiving, learning to hang-glide, playing on adult softball teams, learning to play a musical instrument, traveling more…and the list goes on. We want a diversion from our hectic day-to-day schedules, and quite frankly, we all need diversions. It is all part of the re-energizing process, part of recharging our batteries. However, sometimes what starts out as a leisure pursuit turns into an all-out obsession that actually adds stress to our lives if we don't manage it properly. How does this happen?

Well, like so many other things in life, it just happens; when it does, we create a new set of problems for ourselves. Now, what was meant to be a leisure activity that might help relieve the tensions and pressures from our normal workday, becomes so important and demanding that it actually creates more stress in our life.

A classic example of this is the fitness runner who begins running to do just that, stay fit. From sedentary office worker, our friend progresses from a walking program to running two miles every morning. Then, he decides to enter a 5-k race (three and one tenth miles) and he begins his formal training program. After successful completion of his first race, he's hooked on the recognition and the feeling he felt running through that finish line area. So, he steps up the program, decides to go for longer distances, and eventually finds himself tracking everything in his life so that it contributes to running. He runs twice a day, measures all quantities of food ingested, monitors his heart rate and his hours of rest and in doing all this, manages to ignore his wife, his kids and lose interest in his job. You get the idea.

I know about this syndrome because I've had what I would call partial obsessions or marginally fanatical attractions. Mine have included running marathons, men's ice hockey and mountain climbing. I went through this kind of thing with running, progressing from running just to stay fit to running nine full marathons including both the New York City Marathon and the Boston Marathon. I did it again when I first began to play ice hockey as an adult (I played as a kid) and became consumed with anything and everything that had to do with ice hockey. Then in 1998, I read John Krakauer's best seller, *Into Thin Air,* which detailed the disaster on Mount Everest in 1996. Then I went and saw *Everest* at the IMAX theatre and said, "That's it, I'm gonna go climb a mountain!" So, I immersed myself in mountaineering books and magazines and the like, and in July of 1998, I successfully reached the summit of Mount Rainier. Now, at age sixty, I still run and play ice hockey and yes, I have looked into doing several more climbs, but I am not totally locked into any of these activities quite the way I was when I first got into them. What was I trying to prove?

By doing these things, by proving to myself that I could run 26.2 miles or by playing ice hockey with men twenty years younger than I was, or climbing Mount Rainier, did I find some sense of satisfaction and fulfillment? Well, yes, I certainly did. When it was done, however, when the marathons had been run, when the hockey tournaments ended in either victory or defeat, when I safely got down from Mount Rainier, there was always one question to be answered: Okay, what next? These accomplishments were merely landmarks, stops along the way. They did not provide a final destination, an end point, so why did I ever think I might find some sense of security through these kinds of activities? It mattered, but it didn't matter.

Now, as I look back on it all, I realize a valuable lesson I needed to learn, and one that I wish someone would have shared with me earlier in life. The lesson? Simply put, if your *primary* aim in life is to do nothing but *prove* yourself, you will, sooner or later, run into trouble. The sooner in life that this happens, probably the better.

We often do things in life because we want to prove that we can do whatever it is we are attempting, and in succeeding, confirm something to ourselves. Proving oneself has to do with drive, determination, winning, material gains, position and status. These are words that most people with a Type A personality are very comfortable with. I know this because I am one of those people. Those words reflect things like commitment, self-discipline, perseverance and other noble, honorable virtues. But there is a major difference between *proving* oneself and *being* oneself. Being oneself is about accepting and understanding who you really are. It's about learning to *let go* of the baggage and stupid things we need to let go of. Being is about quality of life issues and looking for, finding, and enjoying the simple pleasures that life has to offer. Being oneself is about honesty, about being *real,* and learning to be content with who you really are. More than anything else, it's about being at peace with yourself.

For most men, myself included, this does not come easy. It is directly the opposite of what we were taught as we were growing up. But if proving ourselves through deeds and acts is not where we will find our security, where should we look to find it? Aren't our lives supposed to be about fulfilling certain ambitions and achieving specific goals? Well, in part, maybe, and then again, maybe not. Let me share a very personal insight I have gained related to the marathons I have run in my life.

In 1980, at twenty-nine years of age, I ran my first marathon. I was working for IBM at the time and with the obligations of my work and my young family, I never properly trained for it. But I was young, fit, a former college athlete, and very strong-willed. So, I went there to prove something to myself, and okay, maybe a few other people who didn't think I could do it. I successfully completed that first marathon in four hours and nine minutes (4:09), averaging nine minutes and thirty seconds (9:30) per mile. Pretty good, right? Well, not by my standards. Even though I had never run a full marathon, I went there trying to break four hours and didn't do that. In addition, my shoes did not fit properly (too tight) and I ended up with blood blisters under all ten toe nails, which allowed me to make a major fashion statement whenever I wore sandals the next summer. Also, I could hardly walk for the next week and actually had to go down stairs backwards because my thighs were so badly beat up from the pounding of running 26.2 miles. So, at twenty-nine years of age, I was disappointed in my performance and my body's ability to recover. Two years later, I did run the same marathon in three hours and forty-nine minutes (3:49) which was my personal best but had a similar two-week recovery period. So much for proving myself as a marathon runner.

Now, let's go to November 4, 2001. I am now fifty years old. It's a beautiful, crisp, sunshiny Sunday morning, and I find myself standing on the Verrazano Narrows Bridge in Staten Island with thirty thousand other runners waiting for the start of the New York City Marathon. Once again, I am marginally trained, and in this case I have not run a marathon in five years. This will be an extremely emotional NYC Marathon since it comes on the heels of the September 11 terrorist attacks on the World Trade Center. Mayor Rudy Giuliani addresses the runners over the loud speakers, telling us that today we are all New Yorkers and it is our turn to embrace the city! In a pep talk the rival of any I ever heard in my college football playing career, Rudy whips us into a frenzy and people are wildly cheering, "high-fiving" one another and clapping. Mayor Giuliani's comments are followed by the playing of the *Star Spangled Banner* and the singing of *God Bless America* and then, as the starting cannon is fired, Frank Sinatra's *New York, New York* blares out the loud speakers. The runners cheer wildly and simultaneously start singing *New York, New York*. Some of the runners start chanting "U-S-A, U-S-A," and others, I notice, are actually crying. As I start across the Verrazano Narrows Bridge I tell myself that I have already experienced something that has made the entire trip to New York City worthwhile. I run, and then I walk, I run some more, I walk some more, and so I go. I wave to people along the route (three million spectators according to the estimates in *The New York Times*), high-five little kids that have come out to watch, shake hands with members of FDNY, New York's bravest, and NYPD, New York's finest. And as I run up mile 26, there is my beautiful, smiling wife with one of our dearest friends cheering me on and taking my picture. Finish time: five hours and forty-three minutes (5:43), just over a thirteen-minute-mile pace. The slowest marathon I have ever run in my life but without question, the greatest experience I have ever had running a marathon. I finish without a blister on my feet and I workout just three days following the marathon. Nothing to prove anymore. But, to be there, to experience what I experienced that day, no one can ever take that away from me. It was an incredible human experience.

Sometimes it's not so much what we do but what we learn about ourselves in the process of doing. In other words, while a very important part of life is about *doing,* about accomplishing certain things, an equally important part of life has to be about *being,* about accepting oneself and honestly facing who we really are. Through some of my experiences, I have come away with a very different perspective of myself, of who I really am, and a lot of that had to do with what I had learned about myself in the process of doing.

For example, over the years, I have learned to laugh at myself and not take myself so seriously. When I climbed Mount Rainier, I learned I could still be frightened and have feelings of uncertainty and insecurity. I also have come to the realization that I am not really in control of my life the way I once thought I was. It really is amazing how many people go through life thinking they are in complete control over their lives and their destiny, when in fact, none of us are ever really in control. At least, not the way we think we are.

Some people will tell you that living life is about taking risks. Now, that does not necessarily mean having blatant disregard for your own personal safety nor does it mean having to run the odds against some sort of death wish. Taking risks can be as simple as *stepping outside of yourself to let others know who you really are.* It's about honesty and being who you really are without being concerned of what others might think of you because of your actions or behavior. Taking risks can be as simple as laughing out loud like a child when you are with a group of adults or sharing your innermost fears and feelings of insecurity with another person, knowing that you may be judged because of those feelings. It can be the simple act of admitting when you have made a mistake, or learning something new from someone and acknowledging that you really are not as smart as some people might think you are. It can be lending a hand to a stranger or, again, something as simple as crying if the moment so moves you. For many of us, maybe the biggest risk of all comes when we stop trying to *prove* ourselves through what we do and instead, begin to make the conscious effort to understand and accept who we really are. Once we understand and accept who we are, we can then *be* who we are.

Maybe our fixation with the activities we choose to take part in has nothing to do at all with finding our sense of security. Instead, maybe it goes back to the child within all of us. That innocent little kid who has an insatiable appetite for excitement and new experiences that is fed by both curiosity and the need for approval.

George Sheehan, the master philosopher of running, once said, and he was speaking of adults when he said it, "Without play, without that child still alive in all of us, we will always be incomplete. And not only physically, but creatively, intellectually and spiritually as well."

I read this quote and thought about Billy's grandfather. A

playful guy, he seems relatively happy in life. He is creative, caring, loving, and knowledgeable of certain things but still, silently questions himself about his own life. Yet, he has this wonderful faith, a certain belief, that maybe tomorrow will be even better than today. Overall, he seems like a pretty complete person.

I wonder if the same can be said for us?

PART III

The Other Missing Peace

Chapter 9

❧

What Should We Really Be Looking For?

In the previous section of this book we examined many of the different ways we try to achieve, create or search for some semblance of security in our life. I believe that the sense of security we would all like to have in our lives is a general feeling that we are in control, that our fate is determined solely by the choices we make and the actions we take. We all want this certain assuredness that says everything's going to be all right. And yet, somehow, for whatever reason, our world doesn't work that way.

In reality, we are not the ones in control. We can and will make certain choices and decisions and we will take appropriate actions based upon those decisions. However, in the end, we come up short. We never seem to find that total sense of security and assuredness. Education and learning, professional success and financial gain, relationships, marriage, parenting and even our individual pursuits, none of these bring the guarantee we are looking for. None of these get the job done. In reality, there is no security or guarantees in our world — not today, not yesterday, nor will there be in the future.

This is not all that easy to accept. Earlier in my life, I fooled myself. I was living with a false sense of security, though I thought it was real. Since then I have learned a lot. I have even learned that the security I thought I saw in my parents when I was a child was as false as my own. Life may have been simpler in some regards, but they had no guarantees in life either.

This raises yet another question for us. If we cannot find *real security* in our world, what then should we be looking for in the course of our lives? Is there something worth having, something that will give us feelings of fulfillment, of being worthy, and the confirmation that each of us does really matter?

In our story "The Missing Piece," Billy's grandfather creates a wonderful lesson for his grandson around nothing more than a missing piece of a jigsaw puzzle that they had been working on for most of their day together. The lesson explained how all our lives are like puzzles and that, over time, they come together to make their own picture. He also explained to his grandson that the people in our lives are the pieces that make up our puzzles and that each piece — each of us — has value, promise and potential. He wanted Billy to know that as individuals, each of us is important, that we do matter. He also talked about how we all are *connected* in a mysterious way, even to people we do not directly have contact with. While Billy had some difficulty grasping this concept, as maybe some adults would as well, the really important point that cannot be overlooked is that in life we are all, somehow, connected to one another. Unfortunately, how often do we ever stop to realize the significance of that?

Think about the analyses we discussed in Part II. As we examined all the different ways we try to find this sense of security in our lives, how much time did we give to the issue of being connected to others? Really, how much time did we spend examining the impact we have on others around us? Isn't that what Billy's grandfather was talking about? How *who we are* and *how we treat others* impacts not only our puzzle but theirs, too?

Our examination in Part II made one thing very clear. We are much more focused on ourselves, our ambitions as individuals and what matters to each of us as we go about living our everyday lives in this world. Whether it is our academic pursuits in the quest for knowledge or our professional lives, we tend to look at these endeavors only from our individual perspective. Even when it comes to our personal relationships, marriage, or being a parent, we tend not to look at relationships from the other person's perspective as much as we do from our own. Again, there is this overriding tone that keeps saying, "What's in it for me? Where will I find my security?" Most of us tend to look at the world through our own eyes and experiences, thinking only of how it impacts me, myself, and I. We are egocentric

Maybe this isn't so unusual. After all, most of us live our lives in our own little self-absorbed worlds. We go about our daily routines kidding ourselves, thinking we are the ones in control. We often take ourselves too seriously and believe we know what is right and what is wrong, and of course, we are always right in both our thoughts and actions. We are in charge, in control, and we know how the game is played. We like to think we are safe, secure and on top of our game day in and day out.

But, deep down, deep down inside ourselves, deep in our souls, we know who we really are. It is here that we honestly admit to ourselves who we really are and accept the fact that we are not in control, we do have shortcomings, and we are not secure with our place in this life. Now, if we live such different lives, presenting one view to the outside world and living our reality deep inside ourselves, how can we ever be at peace? Simply put, we can't.

I believe that many of us in society today are not at peace with ourselves. This may be best exemplified in our self-centered nature as individuals, constantly looking out for number one. We want for ourselves, and our pursuits are almost entirely driven for personal gain. But, more than anything else it is our general lack of trust — or should I say, our inability to trust one another — that illustrates how few of us are at peace with ourselves. If we cannot accept who we really are, if we cannot be honest with ourselves, then how can we ever learn to trust others? Can we even trust ourselves?

I also believe, and have learned, that finding peace in our lives may not be as complex or illusive as we make it out to be. I am absolutely convinced that people can have rewarding, fulfilling lives and find what I refer to as their "missing peace" regardless of education, income, lifestyle, race, color, gender or creed. It is not so much a function of what we do as it is who we choose to be and how we treat other people in the course of our life.

One of the definitions we examined for the word security was freedom from worry. In discussing this definition, we noted that freedom from worry relates more to a mental state and that it is more of an attitudinal issue. Freedom from worry implies that one is secure in his or her knowledge of who he or she really is and what his or her place in life is.

These are people who have honestly assessed their abilities, taken stock of their true strengths and weaknesses and have come to understand and accept their own reality. They also have come to the realization that while no other human being is all powerful over them in their life, they themselves are not in total control. They accept the reality that certain events will occur to them in the course of life over which they have no control. Some of these events may have good outcomes while others can be devastating, but they accept the reality that such occurrences may happen in their lifetime. In addition, because these people have come to such an honest understanding of who they are, acknowledging both their strengths and weaknesses, and the reality of the world they live in, they exhibit a wonderful human quality. They are more open-minded and accepting of others. As a result, they are more willing to reach out to others.

These are the people who have arrived at an understanding that they truly have something inside them that no one can take away. They have found something in their lives that so many people in this world long for. They have found *the real missing peace*.

This is what we will examine in the final three chapters of this book.

Chapter 10

Learning to Give Is Learning to Live

It really is quite simple. *When we learn to give, we learn to live.* This is where we begin to find our missing peace.

Real living is about giving — giving of ourselves to benefit others. It may be our time, our talents, a helping hand to someone less fortunate than ourselves, or in the form of financial gifts. This is what *real* living is all about. When we focus more on what we can do for others than we can do for ourselves, our entire perspective on life changes. It is the first step to finding the missing peace.

This is nothing new. There is an ancient Chinese proverb that says, "The wise man does not lay up his treasures. The more he gives, the more he has." The Bible has countless references to the act of giving ("It is more blessed to give than to receive." Acts 20:35) and Winston Churchill once said, "We make a living out of what we get, but we make a life out of what we give." I am certainly not taking credit for nor do I think I am introducing some revolutionary new concept never before discussed. I am merely bringing to the forefront an issue we all need to contemplate and make a daily part of our lives — giving more of ourselves to others.

In Og Mandino's wonderful book, *A Better Way to Live,* he highlights seventeen rules to live by. One of these speaks to the very fundamental concept of giving, of how we treat other people. This rule states:

> *Beginning today, treat everyone you meet, friend or foe, loved one or stranger, as if they were going to be dead at midnight. Extend to each person, no matter how trivial the contact, all the care and kindness and understanding and love that you can muster, and do it with no thought of any reward. Your life will never be the same again.*

Mandino's rule speaks directly to several key elements of giving that we all should try to practice in our lives.

First, the giving of ourselves starts with nothing else but how we choose to treat other people we have contact with. That, in itself, is a form of how we give to others. Second, we should be giving regardless of who it is we have contact with — friend or foe loved one or stranger. And last, giving, *real* giving, only occurs when it is done with no thought of reward or recognition. When we give of ourselves, from our hearts, it can only be because we want to give. We should never expect anything in return.

What an incredible world this could be if each of us tried to live by just this one rule. Can you imagine how this simple rule, if practiced consistently by everyone, might change our world as we know it? Our interactions with strangers, friends and foes, would suddenly take on new meaning and would fill our lives with positive, meaningful experiences. There would be less stress in our lives, and relationships based on honesty and trust would flourish. People would be more patient with one another, more caring. Husbands and wives would be more understanding with one another and divorce rates would plummet. Crime would virtually eliminate itself by the fact that no one would ever commit a criminal act against another human being. Race relations would no longer be an issue, as everyone would choose to treat everyone else around them with respect and dignity regardless of race, color or creed. The possibilities are endless.

This is not, however, the world we live in nor will it ever be the ideal place I have just described. Unfortunately, there is no way we can get everyone in this world to practice this rule in his or her daily life. So, what are our choices? The answer is simple: We can each make the choice for ourselves. If everyone else refuses to practice this rule in their encounters with the people they interact with every day, that is their choice. On the other hand, each of us can at least make the choice for ourselves and practice this rule in our own lives. If we choose to take this first step, think of how different our own worlds might be.

Giving is such an honorable thing to do. When we give, we are reaching outside of ourselves and saying, "Hey, this other person is more important than my own interests." It is interesting, however, that when we give, when we truly give from our hearts, we find that somehow we get even more in return. I do not mean this in the financial sense. If that were one's purpose for giving, they would not be giving from their heart. I'm talking about intrinsic rewards, wonderful feelings of joy, of self-worth, of acknowledging that we were willing to give of ourselves to benefit others. There is no other way to get this kind of feeling.

When I think about giving and these kinds of rewards, the intrinsic feelings we get from giving, I think of what I will always believe is the most honorable profession in the world, the teaching profession. I can still name every one of my elementary school teachers from kindergarten through the sixth grade, and I can name at least another twenty, maybe thirty, teachers I had throughout my junior high and high school years. Teachers give of themselves every day with the hope that their efforts can make this a better world in which we live.

Teachers do not, in my opinion, get the respect or the appreciation they should. In the past, I had heard the expression that if you couldn't do anything else, you became a teacher. If that was true, I never had any of those teachers when I was growing up. The teachers I had were competent, capable, dedicated, caring people and I will always be thankful for their efforts on my behalf.

When I lived in Florida, I used to jog almost every day and one route took me past a particular garden in a park. In the middle of that garden was a sign that read, "All of the flowers of all the tomorrows are in the seeds of today." I loved that sign, those words. I do not know to whom to credit the quote, but how true it is and what marvelous wisdom is in those words. Teachers, people who dedicate their lives to helping others learn, are the gardeners that tend to the seeds that will indeed be tomorrow's flowers.

There is a wonderful public service announcement for the teaching profession that I have heard on the radio that does a wonderful job of expounding this simple truth. A young boy is talking to his father and the young boy says, "Daddy, when I grow up I'm going to be a teacher."

The father replies, "But son, I was hoping that maybe you'd grow up to be a doctor."

The child answers his father with the words, "But Daddy, if there weren't any teachers, where would the doctors come from?"

So much for the idle statement, "Well, he is only a teacher." Only a teacher? If it were not for our teachers, where would any of us be in our lives? Teachers are true givers and we should always respect them, honor them, and be thankful for their dedication.

Why can't we all strive to be teachers — teachers of positive values, of the importance of self-discipline, of the importance of respecting our neighbor and caring for those less fortunate? Why can't we all be teachers of love and kindness, teaching our children that the world isn't all about what you get in life but about who you choose to be and how you live your life? The truth is, we are these teachers. Our children see us every day and learn by our example. And, unfortunately, the example we set isn't always a good one.

Our children, and all of us, recently learned by the example set by a group of very dedicated individuals. We learned how some people will give of themselves to benefit others, even if it means sacrificing their lives to do so. On September 11, all of us came away with a new set of heroes in our hearts. As the World Trade Center collapsed killing thousands of innocent victims who were trapped in the doomed buildings, hundreds of firemen, policemen, and emergency rescue workers who had arrived on the scene were killed as well. These individuals were literally going up into those buildings in hopes of saving others when everything else in their world came crashing down on them. They didn't stop to ask, "Well, should I do this or shouldn't I?" They had no hesitation, no second thoughts. They reacted on instinct and out of a sense of duty and commitment that had become second nature to them. They understood that when someone else was in trouble, regardless of the situation or who it might be, they were obligated to do everything humanly possible to help that person, to give of themselves, and if necessary, put themselves in harm's way to do it. On September 11 they paid the ultimate price and in doing so, set an example for all Americans and the rest of the world. We will never forget the example they set for all of us, their bravery, their courage and their sense of duty.

As a child, I was very fortunate. I had wonderful parents who set a good example for me and taught me many important values. Among those was the importance of giving. We were not a wealthy family, so my parents did not really have the means to be philanthropic from a financial perspective, but they gave of themselves in many other ways.

My parents were one of five families who founded a community church in our township, a church they felt would benefit the entire community. They actively recruited new families to join the church and my dad was active on the church board serving as treasurer. He also was active in coaching youth sports in our community, and he coached my brothers and me and many of our friends when we were growing up. When I see some of those friends today, many of them comment to me how my dad had influenced them in such a positive way when they were growing up. He gave of himself in the ways he could.

My mother was always giving to others in some way, shape or form as well. If someone in the neighborhood was sick, my mom would prepare a meal for their family and take it over to their house. If one of her friends was having a problem of some kind, she always wanted to know what she could do to help.

For years, my mom used to take this woman on our street who was about eighty years old, out for breakfast once a week. Wind, rain, snow or shine, my mom would faithfully show up at this lady's home every Thursday morning. She would then help this lady with her walker to the car, drive her to the local mall, and help her from the car into the mall for their McDonald's breakfast together. When they were done with their breakfast, they'd sit in the mall and people-watch, try to figure out why the price of the patty melt at Denny's had gone up so drastically and solve other assorted world problems. My mom would then return home by about 10:30 A.M. totally energized and head off to either the church for some committee meeting or to go sell her Avon cosmetics. Interestingly, my mom wasn't any spring chicken herself when she was doing all this. She was in her mid- to late-sixties.

I would ask myself, "Why do all that? What a hassle!" But, my mom was a lot smarter than I was and she had found a certain peace that I couldn't even begin to comprehend at that point in my life. My mom loved her Thursday mornings maybe more than any other morning of the week, except Sunday when she headed to church. I remember asking her once, "Mom, as busy as you are, why don't you bag some of this stuff, especially trying to get that poor old lady to McDonald's for breakfast once a week?"

Mom was quick to tell me she was going to do her Thursday morning breakfasts with her elderly friend for as long as she could. I didn't understand what she was saying at the time, but as I have gotten older, it now is very clear to me. Obviously, her Thursday mornings were as important to her as they were to her elderly friend and it is easy to see why. Those Thursday morning breakfasts gave my mom something to look forward to. When she gave of herself in this way, she felt important, she knew she had value. Simply put, her presence in her dear friend's life was important to her and made her feel better about who she was.

I did learn from my parents' example and during what was one of the most painful periods of my life, I found a sense of healing as I began to care more about other people and give more of myself in the process. Giving can bring wonderful feelings of self-worth, of having value, of being someone that matters; but these feelings become even stronger, more intense, when we reach out to total strangers.

It was 1989 and I had just gone through my first divorce and was trying to make sense of what was then my broken life. I was traveling on business and staying at a hotel in Springfield, Illinois, where I would be calling on a bank the next morning. At about 11:00 P.M. one night, I noticed a bit of a commotion in the hotel's video arcade room as I was walking through the lobby. It seemed that a security guard, who was about sixty-five years old, was having a bit of a problem getting three teenagers to leave the arcade which was now closing. Not being shy, I walked over and said, "Is there a problem here, officer?"

"No," he replied, "just some youngsters who don't know when it's time to quit. I'm going to walk them off the property right now."

I looked at the three boys — dirty clothes, sloppy in appearance, long hair and unsightly facial hair that resembled adolescent attempts at mustaches and goatees. The boys shuffled by us and said nothing. The security guard turned to me and said, "I got this covered. I'll take it from here."

But I didn't like the looks of the situation, so I said, "You know, I could use some fresh air. I hope you don't mind if I walk with you?" and I joined him as the boys went out the front door about ten steps ahead of us.

Once in the parking lot, the boys walked more briskly and started to joke with one another. They snickered at whatever it was they found so funny. Once they had left the parking lot and crossed the street, they immediately turned around and began to call the security guard and me every obscenity you could think of. Grabbing their crotches, making obscene hand gestures, they were as foul-mouthed as any teenagers I had been around in a long time. Finally, they turned and went on their way. The old man turned to me and said, "What a bunch of derelicts!" And, I have to admit, I agreed with him.

As I went up to my room that night, I thought about the three boys. Why were they so angry? What had them so ticked off to the point of giving an old security guard a hard time and then blasting us with obscenities the way they did? Were they always like that? Is that really who they were? Where were their parents and where did these boys live? What was going on in their lives right now?

The next morning I was in the hotel's restaurant drinking coffee and reading the morning paper. I looked up to see the crowded restaurant filled with business people. Then I saw them. There on the other side of the restaurant were the three derelicts I had encountered the night before — same dirty clothes, same sloppy appearance, each with a cup of coffee in front of them. I called my waitress and told her to tell the boys they could order anything they wanted off of the menu. I also instructed her to tell them they had a friend in the restaurant who wanted to buy them breakfast, but she could not tell them who it was.

I went back to my newspaper and only glanced at the boys occasionally. Pancakes, a Belgian waffle and steak and eggs were delivered to their table. As they ate, they curiously looked around the restaurant, trying to solve the mystery. Suddenly, one boy made eye contact with me, then quickly looked away. As he continued to look away from me, it became apparent that he was telling his friends that the guy who had helped the security guard the night before was in the restaurant. Suddenly, all at the same time, they decided to stare at me, I guess, in an act of intimidation. I smiled back at them, nodded my head, and got up to leave.

As I walked by their table I said, "Boys, I hope you enjoyed your breakfast," and I just kept walking. As I finished checking out at the front desk, I turned to see the three boys standing in the lobby.

They approached me and one of the boys asked, "Can we talk to you?"

"Sure." I said, "what do you want to talk about?"

The tallest of three boys spoke first, "Are you a cop?"

"Nope," I replied, "why do you ask?"

"Well, last night you immediately got involved with the security guard who was kicking us out of here and then, this morning, you buy us breakfast. That doesn't make sense. Who are you and what kind of game are you playing?"

Apparently, they thought I had some sort of agenda and they

clearly wanted to know what it was. So, I asked them, "Do you guys have about fifteen minutes?" When they answered yes I said, "Let's go over there where we can sit down and talk for a few minutes."

We sat down and I began to talk to them about the incident the night before. I told them that the security guard is probably doing that job part-time to make ends meet, and the last thing he ever wants is a confrontation or a problem like he had encountered with them the night before. I asked them if they had grandparents. They nodded their heads and I said, "Hey, that guy is probably somebody's grandfather. Now, how would you feel if someone treated your grandfather the way you guys were treating him last night?" They looked down at the floor and then at each other. They got the message.

I then asked them what they were doing in the hotel's video arcade room at 11:00 P.M. on a school night and why they weren't in school now. All of them said they had dropped out. I asked them why and how they thought they were ever going to make it in this world without, at minimum, a high school education. I did everything I could to counsel them in a positive, caring way with the hope they might see that they each had value and it was important that they realize it. I wanted them to see that even I, a total stranger, cared enough about them on this one morning of their lives to at least buy them breakfast and talk with them about what is important in life.

We ended up spending almost thirty minutes together, talking. As our conversation ended, I asked them to make me two promises. First, I asked each of them to apologize to the security guard the next time they saw him. Second, I asked them each to at least consider getting back in school. As I got up to leave, they shook my hand, smiled and thanked me.

Now, for all I know, my efforts might have totally been in vain. Those three kids might have left the hotel that morning and said, "What a sucker!" I have no idea how they really felt about our conversation, my comments, and the many questions that I asked of them. But that's okay. I did what I did because I thought it was worthwhile and the right thing to do at the time.

I took the chance to reach out, to give of myself, and my reward was something I never could have bought. I was on an incredible high the rest of the week, at a time when my life was in turmoil. I cannot describe the feelings I had inside, but they were wonderful. Suddenly, I had value again. I mattered. I felt good about myself for doing what I did. I remember thinking to myself as I drove to my sales call that morning, "I wonder if this event, my intercession with those three boys at this moment in their life, was one of the reasons God put me on this planet?" Regardless, the whole incident proved to be an amazing, inspiring, learning experience for me.

Today, I cannot even remember what bank I was calling on that day or what happened in the sales call, but I will always remember my breakfast and sitting down with those three boys. I hope, and pray, that maybe something I said that day, something I did, a question I asked, anything, might have in some small way made a difference for one of those three boys' lives. But no matter what the outcome might be, I had given of myself in my own way and in return had received so much more. This is the gift we all receive whenever we choose to give.

We don't really begin to live in our lives until we look outside of ourselves, outside of our own personal interests, and experience the joy of giving. When we do this, we begin to find our missing peace. The real beauty of giving is that it can be done anywhere at any time in so, so many ways, and for so many others — your spouse, family members, co-workers, neighbors, or sometimes even better, total strangers.

When we do reach out to give to others, we actually give so much more than what we see on the surface through our act of giving. Giving can bring hope to someone who felt hopeless about life or their current circumstances. Our giving can actually help to reconfirm our faith in one another as human beings; that, in general, deep inside everyone, there is good and we need to always look for that good in others and in ourselves. And of course, the act of giving is an outward expression of our love for one another. It says, "I care about you," and what could ever be a more positive message to share with everyone we meet than that?

A number of years ago, I got sucked into one of the many tourist traps in Orlando, this one being a store in a high tourist traffic area that specialized in genealogy. Of course, once inside this retail operation, they entered your last name into a computer and out came a total printout that supposedly traced your ancestry back as far as some four or five hundred years. The printout was well written and included such items as the names of famous relatives in your family's ancestry and famous events in history that members of your family had participated in. It also described and displayed your coat of arms along with your surname's family motto, written in Latin.

I could see this was a lot of hype and was not impressed. Our coat of arms was really quite ugly, a black background with three yellow crescent moons and a rooster that looked more like Godzilla. However, having studied Latin for two years in high school, I had a special appreciation for our surname's family motto, *Omni Bonum de Donum*. What a wonderful family motto to have. Simply stated, it means, "All Good from Giving." I liked it.

As a matter of fact, I liked it so much that I ended up buying the deluxe tourist package for $279! I bought the official framed certificate, two plaques, four coffee cups and golf shirts all displaying our ugly family crest (you know, the one with the rooster!), all because I loved our family's motto.

Today, those coffee cups are all gone, having either died a slow death in a dishwasher or a more sudden end as they fell to the kitchen floor. The golf shirts? Well, they weren't of the best quality. When I sent them to my brothers as Christmas gifts, they both called me wanting to know what the punch line was. They obviously were not impressed. I believe my two sons still have the plaques, and I think Cory has the certificate. Cory keeps everything.

But, the words, *Omni Bonum de Donum* are special to my two sons and me. We believed in that motto. We felt it had a special kinship with our family, with my mom and dad, their grandparents. It is something we have always held on to, and something I hope that they hand to their children.

Giving something to your children, to your next generation, can be very special, as was the case with a simple gift I gave my son, Brad, when he went off to college. I wanted to give him something as a remembrance of the occasion but I couldn't come up with anything. Then, the day before we were to take him to school, I grabbed an old paperback dictionary I had in my desk drawer. The dictionary, missing its cover and with duct tape along the spine, was tattered and worn with yellowing pages. It was the dictionary I had bought in the bookstore my freshman year in college (1969).

I wrote a note to my son telling him this was the dictionary I had used while I was in college and had continued to use throughout my professional life. I went on to say that I hoped it would serve him as well as it had served me. The book was twenty-five years old, seven years older than my son.

When we were ready to leave campus after moving him into his dorm, it got pretty emotional. Brad had chosen to attend a university that was an eleven hour drive from home and there would be no weekend visits. This was it. He was leaving home. I handed him the dictionary which I had gift-wrapped and asked that he wait until he had some quiet time by himself to open up the gift. I remember saying to him, "It's nothing special, just something I wanted you to have." On the long, quiet ride home, I thought to myself, Gosh, I wish I could have come up with something better to give him. I missed him already.

One week later, Brad sent me a copy of his first college paper. It was for his freshman English class and he had entitled his paper, "Words of Knowledge." As I read the paper, my eyes welled up with tears. It was about the dictionary I had given him. He wrote about his initial disappointment when he opened the package only to find a battered, beat-up old dictionary. And then, when he learned from the note that this was the same dictionary his father had used throughout his college years, how it became, in his words, "more valuable than a handful of priceless gems." He went on to write in his paper, "The book had been with him since 1969. It had been with him through college. It had been with him when he got his first job. It had been with him when he married my mother. And it had been with him when they had their first child, me. Through all these major events, the book had always been something he owned and could turn to when he was not sure of his own knowledge. And now it was handed to me."

The paper was absolutely wonderful, or as they say on one of those MasterCard commercials, "Priceless!" There were other very touching parts of his paper and, of course, I have saved it and will treasure it always. I don't know what sort of grade he got on it, but for me, it was far better than anything I had ever written or read. I gave him an A+. I was extremely touched. It suddenly dawned on me that he realized I was not giving him a dictionary when I gave him that gift, I was giving him a part of me.

The missing peace is there for all of us. Finding it is not really all that difficult. It starts by making a simple choice, and that choice is to give.

Chapter 11

Practicing Forgiveness in Our Daily Lives

Life is filled with disappointment. All of us at one time or another have had to deal with disappointment of some type. These disappointments may be mild and rather insignificant; others can have major life-changing impact. Interestingly though, most of our disappointments in life are related to the behaviors of other people and how their behavior, in some way, affects us as individuals. We may be disappointed by the actions of our spouse, another family member or a loved one. Then again, it could be a co-worker, our boss, a neighbor, close friend, or maybe even a total stranger. Literally, it could be anyone whose behavior in some way impacts our lives. Regardless, dealing with disappointment is a part of life.

How we choose to deal with these disappointments says a lot about who we are. Have you ever really stopped and examined how you handle your disappointments? Do you confront the person who has wronged you and demand an explanation? Do you try to ignore the incident, passing it off as a minor error in the other person's judgment and just let it go? Or do you completely avoid the issue, stuffing the incident somewhere deep down inside you, choosing to live in complete denial because you feel safer there avoiding any and all confrontation? What if the disappointment is a function of your actions and behavior; do you get upset with yourself? There are a myriad of ways that one can react or respond to disappointment, but one emotion almost always rises to the surface in such situations. That emotion is anger.

Anger is a dangerous emotion. An old French proverb says that anger is a bad counselor. This is, indeed, very true. When we are angry, our emotions often take over and control our actions. In anger, we act totally out of character. We do things that later we wish we had not done. We say things we later wish we never would have said. Anger blinds us, and if it is severe enough, it can eliminate our ability to think rationally.

There is yet another intrinsic danger that comes with anger. If we do not get rid of our anger, if we do not in some way cleanse ourselves of this negative emotion, it can begin to rot and decay inside of us. It begins to take the very worst that is inside us and multiply it. We no longer are just an angry person. We now become a vengeful person, wishing ill will on those who originally were the source of our own anger. This sort of negative thinking will then begin to guide our actions in a variety of ways, none of them positive. When this happens, we have allowed our anger to become the overriding emotion in our life, to take over much of who we are. In the process, we are blinded by anger, and in seeking this vengeance, we hold ourselves hostage. Nobody who lives with this kind of anger in his or her heart or mind will ever find the missing peace. It is impossible.

However, we do not have to live our lives filled with anger and negative thoughts. There is another way to handle our disappointments and the anger we feel toward the people who have wronged us. Most important, not only is there a different way to deal with our anger, but we can also actually eradicate it from our heart and mind so that we can move on in our lives. It is here we uncover the second step in finding the missing peace, that being, *Learning to Practice Forgiveness in our Daily Lives.*

Practicing forgiveness is not as easy as giving. In fact for many people, both men and women, their inability to forgive others and themselves cripples their relationships and their very lives. Practicing forgiveness in our daily lives may be the single greatest act that we can practice with one another as human beings, even greater than giving.

In practicing forgiveness in our daily lives, there are three distinct "acts of forgiveness" that we need to consciously be aware of. First, we must be able to *forgive ourselves* for whatever wrongful act we may have committed. We cannot complete the second and third acts of forgiveness if we do not first start with ourselves. This involves a conscious recognition that we have, in fact, done something wrong. We need to admit and accept that we were at fault, that we were wrong. We need to learn from our wrongdoing so we can avoid making the same mistake in the future, forgive ourselves and move on.

Part of this has to do, I think, with the importance of being able to love ourselves. It has often been said, and accepted by most practicing psychologists and theologians, that if an individual cannot love him- or herself, this same individual will have difficulty accepting the fact that anyone else could truly love him or her. I believe there is a similar truth when it comes to forgiveness. That being, if we cannot forgive ourselves, why would we ever believe someone else would be able to forgive us? In practicing forgiveness, we must start with ourselves. Then, and only then, can we move on to the second act of practicing forgiveness.

Once we have forgiven ourselves, we must then be able to *forgive the person or persons that wronged us* in some way. This does not mean that we condone what they did in any way or that we agree with their actions or behavior. It merely means that we are willing to put the incident behind us and acknowledge to the responsible party that in our heart, while we may have been hurt, disappointed, etc., we forgive them for what they have done.

Some people may see this as a sign of weakness; in reality, it is just the opposite. Gandhi himself spoke the words, "The weak can never forgive. Forgiveness is an attribute of the strong." Many times, the person who has disappointed us realizes the wrongdoing and is struggling with the same issue, but cannot bring themselves to ask for forgiveness in fear that they will be confronted and their plea for forgiveness rejected. This leads us to the third, and probably the most difficult, act of forgiveness.

The third act of practicing forgiveness requires us to *ask the person or persons we have hurt for their forgiveness*. When we do this, when we approach another individual to ask for their forgiveness, it means that we are admitting our own wrongdoing, that we, in fact, made a mistake and are willing to recognize that. This is very, very difficult for many people, especially for many men who cannot get past the male pride that was ingrained in them when they were brought up.

As I have grown older and learned some things along the way, I have come to the opinion that for most men, male pride is truly a double-edged sword. As an asset, male pride is often what drives us to achieve, to work hard, to fight the good fight. A large part of why many of us are good husbands and fathers as providers and protectors is because of the pride we were taught to have. We are proud of our accomplishments and earning the respect from our peers is important to us. There is no denying it. Pride has a lot to do with every man's persona. However, this pride thing, this wonderful asset that drives us to do great things, to be the best we can be, can also be a horrible curse.

It is this same pride that keeps us from forgiving others, from going to those we love the most in our lives and saying, "I'm sorry I hurt you. I was wrong. Will you please forgive me?" We may be afraid and insecure, and maybe with good reason, but it is our pride that tells us we cannot show any sign of weakness or else we are not a *real* man. Unfortunately, this can keep us from ever letting anyone, even the people we love the most, from getting too close to us. Many a man has gone to his grave with a broken heart because he was too proud to practice forgiveness in his life. He could not forgive himself, he could not forgive others, and least of all, he would never admit he was wrong and ask for forgiveness.

It also is extremely important to note that once we choose to forgive someone for whatever they have done, we have to put the issue behind us, completely. That does not mean that we will ever forget the incident or the hurt that accompanied it, but we can never bring it up again as a point of contention with the individual we have forgiven. When we choose to forgive someone for what they have done, we release any feelings of anger and animosity toward that person and we can never resurrect those feelings over this same incident. If we do, we have not really forgiven that person in our heart.

I am a huge proponent of practicing forgiveness in our daily lives. This is probably because of the profound impact that practicing forgiveness has had in my life. I should also mention that my strong belief in practicing forgiveness on a daily basis stems from the fact that I am a man of faith, a Christian, a man who worships a loving God who has the capacity to forgive all men and women. His love, God's grace, goes beyond anything I can understand, but my belief in Him is part of the reason I believe in practicing forgiveness. However, it was not until 1989 that I truly became aware of the precious value and power of practicing forgiveness.

I was going through my divorce at the time. The date was June 15, 1989, my thirty-eighth birthday. I was sitting alone in my house that was for sale, mostly empty rooms with the furniture gone. I was living there alone, my boys already living in a condo with my soon-to-be ex-wife. The four-bedroom house which at one time had been our happy home had become my own prison of sorts. I was confused, angry, hurt — pretty much lost in my life. The divorce would be finalized in five days, on June 20. I opened my copy of *Daily Word,* a daily devotional that I have read for years. As I sipped on my orange juice that morning, I began to read this meditation:

Thursday
June 15, 1989

Forgiveness Enhances the Joy and Fulfillment of Life

I forgive the persons for whom I have held any unforgiveness.

Forgiveness releases all animosity and brings an open and clear mind to whatever I am experiencing now.

Forgiveness assists me in making right choices and prompts loving interaction between others and me. Without worry or doubt to cloud my mind, I experience inner peace. Because my attitude of forgiveness is constructed by harmonious thoughts, my day proceeds harmoniously.

Forgiveness allows Truth to have free reign in my life. I can and do forgive myself for any perceived shortcoming. The realization that a response or action of mine could or should have been different shows increased knowledge. I now am aware of better alternatives. Kinder and wiser responses are evidence of my growing ability to forgive myself and others.

"Forgive us our debts, As we also have forgiven our debtors."
— Matthew 6:12

As I finished reading the meditation, tears rolled down my cheeks. I wiped my eyes and read the meditation again. I have since been told that whenever you read anything that has significance of any personal nature, it is best to read it twice, once for your heart and once for your head. For some reason, this meditation at this point in my life touched every part of my body.

It suddenly dawned on me that if I truly did believe in a God who can forgive me for all of the sins and wrong doings that I commit in my life (and certainly I have committed them), shouldn't I try to practice this same model of forgiveness? Even if it were only one zillionth, one infinitesimal, immeasurable amount of the forgiveness He offers me, shouldn't I be able to get past my own selfish interests and forgive myself and my soon-to-be ex-wife for the failure of our marriage?

I sat at my kitchen table that morning and I prayed to the God I worship and asked for His forgiveness for the many shortcomings that were part of who I was and had been as both a husband and a father. I also prayed for my soon-to-be ex-wife, the mother of our two sons, and asked that God watch over her always. I also prayed for the safety and protection of my two sons, who no longer would live in the same home with me, and for the strength to still be the best father I could be for them. That morning, June 15, 1989, may have been one of the most emotional mornings of my life. But when I rose from that kitchen table and headed out the front door to go to work, the sun never seemed warmer on my face, the world never more beautiful. In my heart I had forgiven myself and my wife, and I could now begin to move on. From that day forward, I have always chosen to carry a *forgiving spirit* in my heart and practice forgiveness in my daily life.

That simple act of praying for my own forgiveness and consciously forgiving my wife for the pain I felt she had brought into our lives (she had asked for the divorce) was like an awakening of sorts. I felt like I had taken a refrigerator off of my back. It was an incredible feeling, uplifting, inspiring and totally cleansing. For all of the wrongs I had committed in my life, I suddenly carried no guilt. I could accept myself once again. I was an okay guy. And as for my wife, I came to the understanding that while losing her in my life would be painful, I needed for her to know I had forgiven her and, hopefully, she would forgive me for my shortcomings as a spouse. When these things happen, it is never a totally one-sided situation. When a marriage fails, two people fail.

Today, I am pleased to acknowledge that Jackie, my ex-wife, and I are still dear friends. While we have both moved on in our lives, I can honestly say she is a wonderful person and someone who will always hold a special place in my heart and my life. I would, as her friend, do anything for her. She was, and continues to be, a loving and caring mother to our two sons; she is hard working, fun-loving and has a wonderful capacity to help others.

Following the death of my mom, Jackie had a calling to become a Patient Care Volunteer for Hospice of the Comforter, a Christian-based branch of Hospice. In this role, she would spend time with terminally ill cancer patients in their homes, allowing other family members to have time away from the home. I remember when she had her first patient following her training as a volunteer, her presence made such a strong impression on the family that when the gentleman died, they asked Jackie to read scripture at the funeral service. She continues to do her Hospice volunteer work today as well as leading a positive, productive life for herself.

I cannot tell you how pleased I am and how fortunate I feel as a result of the fact that Jackie and I have been able to sustain our relationship as special friends to one another. Considering that we spent more than twenty-three years of our lives together as husband and wife, doesn't that only make sense? For many people who have been through divorces I know it doesn't, but that is the beauty and power of forgiveness.

I really struggle today when I hear men or women bad-mouth their former wives and husbands. Think about it? What does that say about the person doing the bad-mouthing? After all, didn't these two people at one time feel so in love with each other that they pledged their love and faithfulness to one another for the rest of their lives? In many cases, did they not come together in an act of love and, in many cases, bring children into this world? And now, he's a "worthless bastard" and she's nothing but an "outright bitch"? What sense does that make?

I think of the many memories, the events that Jackie and I shared in our lives together. We brought two new lives into this world. We nurtured our boys together and watched them grow. As a family, we shared holidays, vacation trips, attended school plays and little league events. We stood together as husband and wife as both my mom and dad were laid to rest, and we did the same when her mom passed away. Now, you tell me, why would I not want to maintain some sort of relationship with this person, even though we could not keep our marriage together? Our healing came from our ability to forgive one another, and I will always be thankful for it.

Unfortunately, I do not believe that our story is the norm; at least, it does not seem to be based on what I hear among my friends and professional colleagues who have suffered failed marriages and have gone through divorces. I feel bad for them because harboring such negative feelings and hostilities toward that other person is incredible baggage to drag around for the rest of your life. In too many cases, it is this baggage, the leftover anger, which leads to irrational thinking and breeds negative thoughts. Ultimately, this results in a vengeful attitude toward that other person. But opening one's heart and mind and spirit to the act of practicing forgiveness can change one's outlook and more importantly, one's life.

I am not saying this is easy. For many people, practicing forgiveness is next to impossible because much of it involves admitting to another person our own faults and failures. I also have had friends tell me, "Forgiving is one thing, but how do you ever forget?" Well, I am not sure you ever do.

Forgiving ourselves, forgiving someone else, and ultimately, asking another person to forgive us is not a way of forgetting the wrongful act. What is done, is done, and cannot be undone. However, when we practice the act of forgiveness, we learn from the experience and, hopefully, so does the person who has hurt us. Practicing forgiveness does not give someone a license to repeatedly make the same mistake over and over again. Also, certain acts may have legal consequences and require an individual to pay a certain price and, in essence, be punished, even though we may have forgiven them for their actions.

As parents, we all suffer many disappointments with our children, just as our parents suffered disappointments with us as we grew up. I believe that it is extremely important to practice forgiveness with our children, especially in these times. Too many times, we are too quick to judge and don't spend enough time letting them know how much we really do love them. They need to hear and know that they do matter, that they have value as an individual and that they have a purpose for being on this planet in this life. They need to know that making mistakes is part of the learning process in life and that even though we may be upset with them initially for something they may have done, we are willing to forgive them.

I think we also need to admit to ourselves and our children that as parents we make mistakes. Overall, I am not sure we do a very good job of this. I would go one step further and add that as parents I am not sure we do a very good job of going to them, our children, and ever asking for their forgiveness when we do make these mistakes. Now, I'm sure many of you would say this is ludicrous, to even think of going to your son or daughter and asking for their forgiveness for something that you have done wrong. However, there can be significant value in doing this for both the parent and the child.

As a parent, we often times think we need to be all-knowing, all-powerful and without fault in the eyes of our children. Well, that's nice, but is this *really* who we are? Is this reality? If this is the image we create for our children, will they ever, in their own eyes, measure up to the standard that they think their parents were? I realize there may be some gray areas on this subject, but I think we need to be more honest with our children as they get older and mature. How can we justify compromising honesty as a virtue in the name of creating a false image of ourselves for our children?

I think it is important that as children get older, they develop a realistic understanding of who their parents really are. As adults, and as parents, we need to admit that we have made mistakes in our lifetime and that in all probability, we will continue to make some mistakes as we continue through life.

This is reality. We are not perfect. We are human, just as they are and it is important that our children realize this when they are old enough to understand and appreciate our honesty on this subject. No one in this world is perfect. If we come off that way to our kids, they will either resent us or feel pressured to live up to standards no one can achieve.

Interestingly, and this will probably come as a surprise to many of you, I believe that having a forgiving spirit in one's heart and practicing forgiveness on a daily basis can have significant benefits in the business world. At least it does, if you want to keep your sanity.

The business world can be absolutely ruthless. I know. As a manager I have laid people off and fired people, and yes, I have been fired. As one of my friends says, "Some days you're the windshield; some days you're the bug." Well, business can be great if you are always the windshield, but typically, it doesn't work out that way. When there is money involved, which is what our free enterprise system is all about, anyone and everyone is fair game. No one can deny the reality that office politics exist whether you work in a Fortune 500 company or day care center.

However, as fast-paced and stressful as the business world may be, we can make a simple choice and change the way we live and act. We can choose to either go about our responsibilities with a forgiving spirit in our hearts, forgiving those around us and letting go of the useless baggage, or we can choose to live by a what's-in-it-for-me attitude. To choose the second may bring financial gain, status, power and influence, but it will never provide any semblance of peace for the individual. As mentioned earlier in the book, many people in the business world have made the choice to live by the motto, "He who dies with the most toys, wins!" when the reality is, "He who dies with the most toys, still dies!" As we get older, we discover that the best things in life aren't *things* at all.

When I talk about forgiveness in the workplace, I am not talking about breeding or tolerating mediocrity or incompetence. People need to be given responsibilities and ultimately held accountable for their performance. I understand the responsibilities that go with running a corporate entity efficiently and profitably. However, all of us are human and even with the best training programs and the best processes, mistakes will be made. That's the nature of business; that's the nature of life! So, we have a choice as to how we deal with each other when these mistakes are made.

We can approach the problem as an opportunity for learning and improving future process and address the issue with a forgiving spirit in our heart. Or, we can overreact, look to place blame, threaten, berate and give countless other negative responses that do little, if anything, to improve the situation. We need to always remember and accept that we are all human, and even the best will make mistakes from time to time.

I believe having a forgiving spirit has helped me in my business career and actually made me a better businessperson. Making the choice to practice forgiveness has allowed me to be more open and honest with whomever I have come in contact with in the course of my business dealings — the manager I report to (my boss), the people I manage, my peers, customers, members of the trade press, literally anyone I had to deal with. Once I chose to carry a forgiving spirit in my heart, I could deal with these people with total honesty and openness.

Now, when I make a mistake in my professional life, I am not afraid to admit to it. This is because I have accepted that I am human and I am not ever going to be perfect. Yes, I am going to make mistakes. I know that I will be able to forgive myself for whatever I have done and I will, hopefully, learn from the mistake. Also, in openly admitting to mistakes I have made, I have come to learn that my co-workers respect me more for my honesty and see me as being more *real* and someone they can trust. If anything, this has strengthened my relationships with these people.

I also learned to forgive others around me for things they may have done that impacted me negatively. Regardless of what their agenda was, or their intent, I learned that it was far better to forgive and move on than to weigh myself down brooding about the situation and holding on to intense feelings of anger that would negatively impact my own behavior and productivity. Over the course of my business career, I have learned that there were certain people I could not trust. That did not mean, however, that I should not forgive them for whatever they had done. I believe in the power of forgiving people, that it heals and strengthens relationships. Just because I chose to forgive others does not mean that I allowed myself to become a doormat. There is a subtle truth in the old saying, "If it happens once, shame on you, if it happens twice, shame on me."

Last, when I have screwed up (as we all do), especially in a way that may be hurtful to another employee, I have learned the importance and value of going to that person and genuinely apologizing. At the appropriate time and in the appropriate place, apologizing to someone you work with is an honorable thing to do. It takes courage; it takes strength. Most importantly, it can have a tremendous healing affect on your working relationship with that person. I have never been disappointed in making the choice to do this. In doing so, I knew that in my heart, I was doing the right thing and, in turn, restored part of my own missing peace. In doing this, I also know that I have earned both the trust and respect of others. I know this because I, literally, have had people come to me and tell me this.

Practicing forgiveness in our daily lives has nothing to do with weakness. To the contrary, it shows courage, strength, self-confidence and character. Maybe more than that, practicing forgiveness shows one's ability to love. Loving each other, genuinely caring about each other, this is one of the fundamental principles of forgiveness. We are all imperfect. We all make mistakes. We make wrongful judgments and poor decisions and those mistakes affect other people's lives. We need to be honest with ourselves and acknowledge our mistakes, our imperfections, our shortcomings, so that we can begin by forgiving ourselves. Then, we can forgive those who have hurt us and ask for the forgiveness from those we have hurt. No, it is not easy, but practicing forgiveness in our daily lives is a critical element of finding our missing peace.

Today, I am a better husband, a better father, a better businessperson and a better individual because I have learned to practice forgiveness in my daily life. Without question, it has been a necessary element in helping me find an inner peace, the missing peace that I never knew could even exist. What an incredible blessing it has been to experience, firsthand, the healing that occurs and the positive feelings one feels when he or she chooses to practice forgiveness in daily life.

In this life, on this earth, the ability we have been given to forgive one another could very well be God's greatest gift to us. It can literally transform your life and the person you are. Maybe of even more importance, practicing forgiveness can help you find your missing peace.

Chapter 12

&

The Need for a Spiritual Foundation
in One's Life

Clearly, when we choose to give more of ourselves to others and carry a forgiving spirit in our hearts, we begin to transform our lives and change who we are in a very positive way. However, we are still missing one essential component that each of us must have if we are ever to truly find our missing peace.

Like the first two components we have discussed, the third is available to each and every one of us, regardless of age, race, gender, color or creed. You cannot buy it because it is not for sale. It has nothing to do with money or social status. It is something that has the potential to enrich our lives beyond all else that we have discussed, and yet will still sometimes leave us filled with wonder, pondering for answers. However, more than anything else that has been discussed in this book, it comes the closest to answering where each and every one us can find our missing peace. I am talking about *the need for a spiritual foundation in one's life.*

More than anything else, each of us needs to have some sort of spiritual foundation in our life if we are ever to truly find peace within our hearts. I believe this because in my own life there have been countless times when I could not find the answers I was looking for and needed a place to turn. Hurting, lost, in times of trouble and concern, where does one turn for the answers, for guidance? How could I, how can anyone, ever come close to finding their missing peace without having a spiritual foundation in their life?

I write this chapter as I have the previous chapters of this book, based upon personal experience. I am not a member of the clergy or some well-schooled theologian who is steeped in the study and knowledge of the various religious ideologies. So, what I write on this subject is largely from my perspective and based upon my experiences, not interpretation of Biblical scripture or specific knowledge related to theology. I am not qualified in those aspects of religious study. I just know that as a middle-aged guy trying to make it in this world, I have needed my spiritual foundation in order to find any semblance of my missing peace. Now, more than ever, I find it hard to believe that anyone can be at peace with themselves if they do not have some kind of spiritual foundation, a rock to stand on, in their life. Why do I say this? Well, let's examine our world today.

Our world is hectic and totally unpredictable. It is raucous, loud, shocking and nothing seems to stay the same. The only thing that is a constant in our lives is the ever-accelerating rate of change. We are bombarded by advertisements on the radio, television and via the Internet telling us what products we need to buy in order to make our lives complete. Like Pavlov's dogs salivating at the sound of a bell, we respond by chasing the almighty dollar, thinking we can buy our dreams and in doing so, forget to live our lives along the way. We achieve great things in our own minds and by our own standards, but for some reason, it's still not enough. We acquire material things and maybe even achieve financial wealth, but then wonder why we still feel such a void in our lives. Technology continues to evolve with estimates saying that compute power is doubling every twelve to eighteen months. While technology has improved productivity levels and introduced many new conveniences into our lives, it now threatens to completely overwhelm us. Ironically, tools that were meant to improve communications, like e-mail and texting, now consume us day and night with an inordinate amount of information, much of which is meaningless. In many respects, one might say these technological improvements now have us choking to death on our own clutter. Is this really the way life is supposed to be? How does anyone make sense of this world today? How can we ever find our missing peace amidst such turmoil?

I recently sat in my car at an intersection when a huge, white tractor-trailer truck made its turn in front of me. As the trailer portion of the vehicle lumbered through the intersection, in bold blue letters on the side I read these words, Delivering the Future — I thought to myself — Is that the next step? Instead of living our lives, maybe someday we will all just order our futures and have it simply delivered to us?

In the book *Anchors for the Asking,* by Harold Hazelip and Ken Durham, the authors very creatively describe how simple life could be if we could order it as though on a restaurant menu. "For an appetizer I'll take the private academy and a full scholarship to Harvard Business School. I'll have the house-in-the-suburbs salad and a cottage-in-the-mountains for my soup of the day. For the main course, put me down for a secure position in a major firm. For my three vegetables, I'll have good health, a sense of fulfillment, and problem-free children. For dessert, give me a condo in a retirement village just west of Disney World." If only it were that simple.

When it comes to our lives and the real world, it is not all that simple. In fact, much to our dismay, we are not in control. Oh, don't get me wrong, our choices have a lot to do with much of what happens to us in life, but we are in no position to order our future. There are and always will be unexpected crises we have to deal with in life. They just somehow happen, and when they do, it becomes even more clear that we all need to have some kind of a spiritual foundation in our life.

Every so often, we get a wake-up call, an event that occurs in our life that forces us to stop and examine how we are living our lives. Suddenly, we realize that our life is not a never-ending proposition and we ask ourselves what really is important. Such events can be of a more personal nature such as a terminal illness, an accident with tragic consequences or the death of a family member or a close friend. Then again, sometimes these events are of such magnitude that they can affect an entire community, city or our entire country.

Every generation has experienced events of this nature. The attack on Pearl Harbor, President Kennedy's assassination, the *Challenger* space shuttle tragedy, the bombing of the *Alfred P. Murrah Federal Building* in Oklahoma City, the shooting at Columbine High School, etc. such events give us all reason to pause and reflect on our own lives. Of course, the most devastating single event to impact all of us as Americans was the terrorist attack that occurred in our country on September 11, 2001. In an instant, not only did our lives change, but the world itself also changed. There was no real warning; no one could even imagine such carnage happening in our world, and of all places, in America? How could this happen? Why did this happen? We all wanted answers. Some people tried to explain the unexplainable by saying, "It must have been God's will," (I will comment on this perspective later) while others asked, "Where is our God?" However, it is when such events occur in our lives, events that force us to contemplate our own mortality, that we often examine how it is we are living our lives. It is also interesting to note that when such events do occur, in our most difficult times, it is God that we turn to hoping for some sort of answer. Why is it that we look to God only in our most difficult times?

The late, great Tony Mason, a former football coach and motivational speaker, used to give a very inspiring speech called "The Ingredients of the All-American." As an extremely successful high school football coach in Ohio and then an assistant coach on the University of Michigan staff, he had been around a lot of All-American football players and said that as he looked back on them, they all possessed four key ingredients or traits. He also said he felt that the real All-Americans in life, the responsible, hard-working, dedicated mothers and fathers who did their jobs to the very best of their abilities, every day, both in the home and in the workplace, also possessed these same four traits. The first of the four ingredients was *spiritual soundness,* a foundation in one's life that guided his or her thoughts and actions as an individual. As Tony would say in his speech, "Be proud of your religion. Speak not against any man."

This statement raises some interesting points. "Be proud of your religion." Religion? A lot of people have very negative feelings when they hear the word: religion. How often do we hear, "Oh yeah, I am a spiritual person. I believe in God, but no, I am not a religious person." Why is this and how is spirituality different from religion?

I think one of the best explanations I have ever read on this controversial subject was in a book entitled, *Who Needs God?* by Rabbi Harold Kushner. In this book, Kushner, talks about an encounter he has with an idealistic college student who is home on vacation. To paraphrase Kushner's words, the student says he believes in God, believes in being kind to people, treating them right, not hurting them, but he does not believe in organized religion. He goes on to say he sees no need for professional clergy, prayer books, organized services and rules and rituals. Also, he laments about why there has to be so many different religions, all arguing about who is right. In the end, the student asks, "Why isn't it enough just to tell everybody to be nice to one another?"

These are pretty good arguments for the position the young man takes. I know these arguments. I have heard them from both of my sons. However, Harold Kushner, a man I would consider to be a knowledgeable, insightful, well-educated theologian, makes two excellent points in responding to the idealistic young man.

First, he agrees that some people can create holiness all by themselves, the way Mozart could create immortal music without ever having taken piano lessons. However, he goes on to say that most of us do need a structure and the company of other people to practice our faith and beliefs together. That somehow, there is a certain strength and comfort that comes in fellowship, the community of worship. Second, Kushner also speaks to the student about the time-tested wisdom of traditions that have been passed down and still exist in this day, literally thousands of years later. He urges the youth to accept what the Jewish religion had learned over time rather than dwell on the mistakes or shortcomings.

I find it interesting how much of our society today mirrors the disposition of the idealistic young man in Kushner's book. So many people today are always quick to point out what is wrong with something, offering no solution to make it better and at the same time, refusing to recognize what good comes from it in its present form. Why do we choose to live our lives this way?

I am not here to condemn or condone organized religion. Speaking for myself, I believe there is a place for both spirituality and religion. However, I think it is important to try and understand how they are different. Spirituality is what provides the foundation for how we choose to live our lives. In many respects, it has to do with the most basic and fundamental beliefs that relate to God, our existence and this universe as we know and understand it. Spirituality may have no ties to a specific religion, and yet it still can provide a person with the basis for how they treat other people and the hope that our world is more than just a cosmic fluke. Religion, on the other hand, speaks more to the adherence of certain specific beliefs and doctrines, and the devotion to a particular faith. In many respects, it further refines one's spiritual foundation by defining more clearly exactly what it is that one does believe in as part of their faith. Religion, by more clearly defining the beliefs and doctrines of a particular faith, provides the structure and order which become the basis for the community of worship that Kushner described.

I think of myself as being both a spiritual person and a religious person. My spiritual foundation has always been very clear to me. I believe that there is a God, one God, and that He is an almighty, omnipotent, loving God whose power goes beyond anything that we can imagine. I also believe that He created this world, that we are not some cosmic fluke on an errant course flying through space, and that He watches over us day and night. His gift to us was this world and the life we live in it, and as a loving God, He wants us to love one another. That is the simplicity of the spirituality that serves as a foundation in my life.

I also have made a choice in my life to further refine that foundation through religion. Simply stated, I am a Christian, a man of faith. I believe in God, and I have accepted and publicly confessed Jesus Christ, His only Son, as my Lord and Savior. Once I accepted this in my heart, it became the spiritual foundation that would guide me for the rest of my life. I knew I could never stray from it. It is my rock, so to speak, and I stand on it firmly.

There have been times in my life when I was, shall we say, more religious than at other times. There have been times in my life when I was an avid church member and actively participated in various programs at the church I was attending. I was more consistent in terms of my active participation, more disciplined in how I practiced my faith. Then, there have been times in my life when I have not been as religious, and I became less disciplined in attending church and actively practicing my faith. Yet even in those times of wandering, I never lost the spiritual foundation in my life. Somehow, like a pilot light that burns unnoticed but is required to light a larger flame, my spirituality, the Christian doctrine that I had accepted and believe in, was always burning in my heart. There was no denying that. As the saying goes, God never walks away from us; we choose to walk away from Him.

As a Christian, I know what I believe. I have studied scripture and have led high school and adult Sunday school classes in some of the churches I have belonged to. I have been active in Baptist, Methodist and Presbyterian churches throughout my adult life and my ex-wife, who was raised in the Roman Catholic faith, and I brought up our two sons in the church. In my life, I have witnessed to others about my faith and the beliefs that I have been taught. Why? For the simple reason, they are what I believe in and they have brought me comfort in times of pain, strength in times of weakness, hope in times of despair, courage when I was afraid. In essence, even though I have suffered the pain of loneliness at certain times in my life, I can honestly say, I have never *really* been alone.

My beliefs, my faith in God, my faith in Jesus Christ are what have helped me deal with the most difficult crises and failures that I have had to face in my life. Therefore, I find truth in my faith and the things I believe in. In sharing those beliefs with friends who were hurting and looking for answers, it was my hope that it might bring them comfort and help them to realize the importance of having a spiritual foundation for themselves in their lives. I have difficulty thinking or believing that it can only be one way, however.

With something as personal and intimate as one's spiritual beliefs, one's spiritual foundation so to speak, why would we, why should we, ever argue about who is right and who is wrong when it comes to such matters?

My younger son Cory asked me a pretty deep question one night when we were out having dinner together. He was about sixteen at the time, at that point in life where most young people pretty much question everything, especially if it resembles any form of authority. Out of nowhere, he comes right at me and says, "Hey Dad, do you think Mahatma Gandhi is burning in hell?" I about choked on my cheeseburger!

Of course, my thought was, Can't we talk about what you're doing in school? Wiping my mouth, I asked if he would please repeat the question, and he did. I did not have a real clear, crisp answer for him on this one. Before I could respond, Cory was quick to point out that if in order to be a Christian and receive the promise of *everlasting life,* one had to accept Jesus Christ as their Lord and Savior, where would that leave Gandhi? "What do you think Dad?" Of course, this was his fun, spirited way of challenging me and everything I believe in.

Being somewhat sarcastic, I think I tried to make light of the question and said something like, "Well, I'm not sure, but I hope he likes toast." But Cory's question led to an even deeper discussion.

Cory shared with me that he had been reading books and studying different religions and ideologies. As a result of his research and reading, he was postulating a theory that while there was only one God, maybe God knew that Jesus Christ would not be enough for everybody in the world. Maybe God knew that the Christian faith would never really speak to the heart of every single person on this planet, even if it were the ultimate truth. Because God is omnipotent, He knew that some would hear a different message, be it the message of Hinduism, Buddhism, the

Islamic faith, the Jewish faith, etc. And since all of the people are God's children, maybe this was how He made sure they all would find comfort in a belief system, a faith, that mattered to them. In other words, while there were different belief systems or religions on our planet, the same God was responsible for all of them. This wasn't my theory or concept; this came from a sixteen year old who obviously was looking for answers about his own spirituality.

This conversation Cory and I had that evening has stayed with me ever since, not because I necessarily agreed with his theory, but because it did make me stop and think about something. It made me think of how many times in my life I have wrongfully judged others for being different than I am, for believing differently, for worshipping differently. It also reminded me of my other son, Brad, and his comments to me about the American Indians he lived with on an Indian reservation in Nevada for ten days when he was a sophomore in college. In American Indian culture, it has been written that many of the tribes believed their bodies to be a "house with four rooms." Within the house, each room was dedicated to a different aspect of the individual. There was the physical room, the mental room, the emotional room and the spiritual room. The Indians believed that every individual needed to spend time in every room, but too much time spent in any one room was considered unhealthy and created an imbalance. Nevertheless, the spiritual room was clearly considered to be the foundation for the American Indian in the house with four rooms.

I remember Brad saying to me after he returned from his trip how poverty-stricken the Indians were and how horrible their living accommodations were on the reservation. However, he was quick to add, "Dad, they were some of the happiest people I have ever been around in my life. They have a very special peace, a spiritual side to them that somehow brings an amazing peace into their lives that satisfies their souls." What an incredible learning experience for my son to have at such a young age in his life. To see these American Indians, young and old alike, living in poverty, yet so rich in spirit. What a strong testimony to the value of having a spiritual foundation in one's life.

As I have studied mountaineering and read about many of the expeditions in the Himalayas, I have been intrigued by the Sherpas, an ethnic group whose nomadic ancestors migrated from Tibet to the Khumbu Valley in northeastern Nepal in the 16th century. The Sherpas are, for the most part, a very poor people, as are many people in Nepal. Many of them live in one-room, stone huts with no running water or electricity. But the Sherpas are a proud people and very strong in the Buddhist faith. Amazingly, despite their poverty and meager lifestyles, they are known for being humble, gracious, friendly and warm. They are dutiful servants. It is the Sherpas who have made it possible for many Westerners to achieve their dream of climbing Mount Everest. Working for as little as seven dollars a day, the Sherpas play a major role in almost every Himalayan mountaineering expedition, serving as porters and cook boys, putting in the routes, and on occasion, saving lives along the way as well.

However, above all else the Sherpas are committed to their Buddhist beliefs. Wherever they go, they take their Buddhist beliefs (and prayer flags) with them, living those beliefs every step of the way. More than just a spiritual foundation, the Sherpas' beliefs guide their everyday actions.

Now, I have cited only two examples, and ironically they are on opposite sides of the world, but here are two groups of people, American Indians and Sherpas, who have little in the way of material goods or financial wealth. Yet, they are people who have found a certain peace within themselves. How can that be in this day and age?

Most of us would probably sit in the comfort of our homes, look at pictures of the deplorable living environments these people endure on a daily basis and think to ourselves, "In this day and age, people really live like that?" Even harder for most of us to imagine is that these people are, generally speaking, happy people, people who somehow have found a certain peace and calmness in their lives. I believe it is because of the spiritual foundation they have in their lives. They have a belief system, a faith, which brings meaning to their lives and their actions.

Looking at these two examples, can we not learn something? One, that there is real value that comes from having a spiritual foundation in one's life; and two, that none of us are here to judge others because of how they choose to worship their God. Why should we even question or challenge the religious beliefs and spirituality that give these people their strength, bring them their comfort and give them their peace? Where they find their peace with their God, where any man finds his peace with God, that is their business. None of us were put on this planet to judge our fellow man.

I feel especially bad for those people, late in their years, who have yet to find any kind of spiritual foundation. I say this for a couple of reasons. One, if they have lived that much of their life without any kind of spiritual foundation, then it would be my guess that they have struggled and have not found much peace along the way. This is unfortunate for anybody. But there is another reason that I feel bad for those people. It is because of something I learned from my ex-wife who does patient-care volunteer work for Hospice of the Comforter. In her volunteer training, she was told, "People die the way they lived." I believe this to be a very true statement.

In other words, our attitude in life and how we choose to live often reflects how we leave this earth in death. People who have lived their lives filled with bitterness and anger, constantly complaining, looking to cheat someone out of something and always trying to be one-up on everyone else, usually have pretty painful, ugly deaths. To the contrary, those who have lived their lives seeking ways to help others and give of themselves, to seek out the best in those they meet, and generally care about other people, usually have more peaceful deaths. Interestingly, my ex-wife has shared with me that in her Hospice volunteer work with terminally ill cancer patients, she has witnessed firsthand the truth of this statement.

Fortunately for my two brothers and me, our parents gave us a very solid spiritual foundation early in our lives. As I have previously mentioned, our parents were actually one of five families who banded together and founded a church in our community. As a kid, however, I didn't like going to church. Who likes to get up early on a Sunday morning, get cleaned up and dressed up when you could be sleeping in or watching cartoons? So, I wasn't exactly drawn to the church and organized religion as a young boy growing up.

But I learned things in that church, even at a young age, things that have stayed with me over the years. I saw people who cared about each other, and I saw healthy and positive interaction among adults and children who were part of families just like mine. I did learn about being respectful and about reverence, and I was taught right from wrong. I also learned about how we all needed to live by something called the Golden Rule: Do unto others as you would have them do unto you. When someone at our church was hurting due to a tragedy or illness, I saw my parents and other people lend a helping hand to help those people. So even at a young age, I learned a number of things, positive things from being involved at our church. But even more important than all those simple lessons of life, I learned about God's grace and how He loved me and cared about me. I learned that our world, our universe, was the result of some omnipotent power that I could not really even begin to appreciate and comprehend as a child. But this presence, the God I learned to worship, was loving, caring and all-powerful, and even as a child, I prayed to Him every night. Little did I know how important this foundation would be later in my life.

My first realization of the importance of this spiritual foundation in my life came when I was twenty years old. I was in my junior year in college at the time. The college years, for many young people (myself included), are typically not what you would call the strongest period in one's life for practicing one's faith and religious beliefs. I cannot really remember going to church or engaging in quiet, prayerful thought much during my early college years. That all changed on Saturday, October 31, 1971.

While watching my younger brother play in a high school football game that would determine their league championship, my dad suffered a stroke. He was only fifty-five years old at the time. I was playing in a college football game that same afternoon and when I got back on campus, I called home to talk to my mom and dad. I remember my mom's voice trembling over the phone when she finally got the words out, "Well, we're a bit upset here. Your dad has had what we believe is a stroke and he is in the hospital." I was devastated by the news. At the time, I didn't even understand what a stroke was. All I knew was that my dad was in the hospital and something was obviously very wrong with his health.

One day later, I received a phone call from my older brother, John, and he told me that dad had suffered a massive stroke during the night and he was now in a coma. His doctors didn't know how long he might live, and I needed to get home immediately. I went to inform my head football coach, Fred Martinelli, who in many ways has been like a second father to me. As I tried to tell him what had happened, I broke down to tears in his office. I couldn't even get the words out of my mouth.

I remember sitting on the airplane on my way home, blankly staring out the window and wondering if my dad would even be alive by the time I got to the hospital in Buffalo. I had broken my hand in our Homecoming game just two weeks earlier and was wearing a plaster cast on it. I would wear the cast all week in practice and then our team physician would take it off on Friday so I could have my hand taped up and play in our game on Saturday. Then, following each game, the doctor would recast my hand in the training room. I looked at the cast on my hand and my thoughts went back to that Homecoming Weekend. I remembered my mom and dad as they got ready to leave campus and head on their way home. Standing in the parking lot next to my dorm, my dad put up his fists like a prizefighter, "bobbed and weaved" a little, landing a light jab to my ribs, and said, "Take care of that hand, Buddy. Drink your milk." Like any father who really loves his son or daughter, even though I was twenty years old, he was still offering loving advice, still caring. I was still his little boy.

When I arrived at the hospital, dad was in a semi-coma, eyes shut, his body was perfectly still in the bed. The deadly silence in the room was punctuated only by the consistent beep of an EKG machine. The setting sun that still peeked in the window cast a warm glow across his bed. I was surprised how peaceful he looked, having no idea what to expect when I got there. His right arm was cold and limp and laid along the side of his body in the bed. I went to the left side of the hospital bed and grabbed my dad's left hand with both of my hands. Suddenly, big tears streamed down my father's cheeks even though he lay there with his eyes shut. I hadn't said a word, but he knew from the cast on my hand that I was at his bedside. I stood there and unashamedly cried like a baby. I kissed his forehead and told him how much I loved him and how much I wanted him to get better. Then I headed down the hall to the men's room, went in, and became physically ill. My emotions had brought me to that point. Never in my life had I seen my father that way, helpless, ill, totally inca-pacitated. I remember asking myself, "What will I do if he dies? How will I manage to get along in my life without him?" He had always been there for me.

Two days later, with our dad showing no signs of improve-ment, my older brother and my mom sat down with me and told me that I needed to go back to school in Ohio. I didn't want to leave, but they told me that if dad was well enough to speak and make his wishes known, that is what he would want. So, reluctantly, I flew back to Ohio on Thursday morning, not knowing if I would ever see my dad alive again.

As fate would have it, that weekend was Parent's Weekend on the Ashland College (now Ashland University) campus. I remember Saturday, November 7, 1971, like it was yesterday. Cold and crisp with the sun shining brightly, it was a spectacular autumn day. As I walked across campus that Saturday morning, parents were everywhere walking the campus with their sons and daughters, taking pictures, hugging, walking arm-in-arm, laughing, smiling. Just two weeks earlier, I had gotten engaged at Homecoming and both my mom and dad and my future in-laws had come down for the game. It had been a special time, a happy time. But today, my dad was lying in a hospital bed fighting for his life and my whole world had been turned upside-down. It was a very surreal experience for me, seeing all my friends and some of the guys on the team with their parents. I kept asking myself, "Why am I even here? I should be home at my dad's bedside."

As I went out onto the field that day for our pre-game warm-up, I thought about when I was a little boy and all the times my dad had thrown the football with me in our front yard at home. I thought about how much he had given of himself to me, so that I could have the opportunities I had. I thought about all the times he had watched me play football and how he had supported me in everything I had done. And then I thought, What will my life be like if he dies?

Then, standing by myself, with the marching band playing as they made their entrance into the stadium, with students and parents filing into the stands, I looked up at the sky and I started to cry. Without even thinking, I knelt down on one knee right there on the 33-yard-line at the south end of the field (I remember exactly where it was) and I prayed. I prayed to my God to make my dad well, but I also prayed for the strength and courage to go forward in life, regardless what might happen to my dad. That was probably the first time in my young adult life I realized the importance of having a spiritual foundation. I knew right then that I was going to need someone a lot bigger than my own dad as I went forward in my life. I had come to the realization that my dad would not always be there for me, and I would still have questions and need somewhere to turn. On that Saturday afternoon, I left my childhood behind and became a man of faith.

Today, I can read any newspaper, watch any television news broadcast, go online on the Internet, and come up with at least a half-dozen reasons why this world is totally screwed up. If I take it all in at face value, ignoring the spiritual foundation in my life, I could say this is one messed up place to hang your hat, a planet pretty much out of control, a lost cause. Based on that assessment, I guess I could adopt an attitude that says, "I'm going to live for the moment, my way, and screw everybody else." Now, if that is how we all chose to live our lives, can you even imagine what our world might be like? How much peace do you really think any of us would ever find in this world, in this life?

I know that there are those who do not believe in any faith nor do they believe in the existence of God. Some people would prefer to go even a step further and admit to the existence of a God but blame Him for all that is wrong with the world. The simplest example of this occurs when there is some type of tragedy that takes the lives of innocent people and in our hopelessness to explain the unexplainable, we all too often hear the phrase, "Well, it must have been God's will."

This is, at best, a feeble attempt to find an explanation and to place blame somewhere when we have no idea where to place it. Everything has to have an explanation, right?

When we cannot explain something, a certain tragedy or calamity, well, it must be God's will. I heard this from more than one individual regarding the events of September 11 as I would discuss the tragedy in the days and weeks that followed with people I came in contact with. But, if that were true, if God actually "willed" that to happen, why would anyone ever want to worship a God such as that?

A good friend of mine, Joe Beavon, who is a former Methodist minister, gave me a wonderful perspective on this subject when I was a young man in my late twenties. He shared his wisdom on this subject in one of his sermon's entitled "Why Me?" The sermon addressed the issue of fate as it relates to God's will and the loving nature of the God we worship. To paraphrase my dear friend, he made it clear that what God *wills* to happen in our world and what God *allows* to happen are two very different things. However, it is when we consider the characteristics that would be *logical* for a loving God to possess that we are likely to make better sense in our quest to understand God's will. When we consider God's will, we need to ask "Why me?" in the context of *all the events of our lives* rather than just the negative and painful ones. When we do this, we can more clearly see and understand God's love as he expresses it to each and every one of us.

Part of the reason we all need to have a spiritual foundation in our life is to help us understand that we will never have all the answers. We never have had them and we never will. We can conduct all the scientific research we want to. We can go to the ocean floor, the farthest reaches of our universe, or break down the human body to its simplest molecular structures; there still will be unanswered questions. No matter where we go, no matter how much scientific research we do, there will still always be questions we cannot answer. Unexplained events, miracles, moments in time that will be marked in history forever; we still will not have the answers.

When it comes to trying to understand our God and the role that His presence plays in our lives as a spiritual foundation, maybe the words found on a simple prayer card say it best:

> *The light of God surrounds me,*
> *The love of God enfolds me,*
> *The power of God protects me,*
> *The presence of God watches over me,*
> *Wherever I am, God is.*
>
> James Dillet Freeman
> 1912–2003

There is an old adage that says the journey is its own reward. I believe in that adage, but one needs strength for that journey. When I was going through my first divorce, I heard a sermon entitled, "Strength for the Journey." It was given by a Presbyterian minister and well-known family counselor in Maitland, Florida, Dr. Richard Brown. In his sermon, he talked about believing in three things, the sovereignty of God, the living presence of Christ in our daily lives, and the power of the Holy Spirit. In closing his sermon, he spoke these words. "When you believe these three things with all your heart and with all of your mind and with all of your soul, then, you will have strength for the journey."

I remember how moved I was by the words of this sermon. I remember saying to myself, "Could it be said any better? Isn't that really what my spiritual foundation is all about, having strength for the journey?"

As I said in the introduction of this book, and now as I come to the close, I certainly do not have all the answers. In fact, while writing this book has been somewhat of a therapeutic adventure for me (as I hope it has been for you reading it), I now find myself filled with even more unanswered questions. But, there is one thing I do believe.

I believe that all of us, at some point in our life, will want to find our missing peace. It may be at different times for different people and all for different reasons, but all of us, at one time or another will probably want to find it. Few of us in this world today are at peace with ourselves, for who we are, for what we do, for who we choose to be and how we treat other people. Oh, on the surface we may justify ourselves and our actions, but deep down, in the darkest reaches of our soul, very few of us are at peace with ourselves the way we would like to be.

When we do come to the end of our days, we will want to know: Did my life really matter? What did I do that was worthwhile and made this world a better place than when I was born into it? Did others love me and did I show love to them? Did I ever find my missing peace?

Whether we find it or not, well, that is a matter that can only be determined by each and every one of us for ourselves. However, if we *give more of ourselves to others,* if we *practice forgiveness in our daily lives* and if we *focus on the spiritual foundation in our life,* we may just find it! And when we do, we may just start to look at our lives and the rest of the world as Billy's grandfather did at Mirror Lake. Do you remember?

"Oh, how I do love this view, this place, this life." Yes, this was a good place to be and this had been a very special day.

Maybe, just maybe, tomorrow would be even better.

Epilogue

Billy hunched over and grabbed his knees. His ice axe in his right hand, he planted it firmly in the snow, rose from his hunched-over position and stood as tall as he could to take in the view. The vista was awesome, much more impressive than what he had even imagined it would be.

He was standing on Columbia Crest, the highest point on the crater's rim that marks the summit of Mount Rainier. At 14,411 feet, he had completed what is considered by many to be the longest and one of the most arduous endurance climbs in the lower forty-eight states. More importantly for Billy, in reaching the summit of Mount Rainier he had fulfilled a life-long dream.

While he was pleased with his accomplishment, he was not overwhelmed with exhilaration or excitement like he thought he might be when he imagined and had so many times dreamt of this moment. There was just a feeling of satisfaction. He had success-fully accomplished something he had always wanted to do; something he had always promised himself that he would do.

Standing there, he looked to the south where he could see Mount St. Helens and Mount Adams. Even further away, he could see Mount Hood. He chuckled to himself, wondering if maybe, somebody, some total stranger he had never met might be standing on its summit looking at Mount Rainier where he was standing. He looked below to the blanket of clouds that hid the rest of civilization from view and realized how much irony there was in this moment. Here he was experiencing the culmination of a lifelong dream, and yet, beneath the clouds, it was business as usual for the rest of the world. He had looked forward to this moment for twenty-three years, ever since he was ten years old when he spent that Saturday with his grandfather making that puzzle. Now, he was realizing the moment and below the clouds, people were going about their own lives, pouring milk over corn flakes, getting the kids ready for school, driving to work, etc. Really, it was just another day.

He took off his gloves, unzipped his parka, and reached deep inside to unzip one of the pockets of his fleece top. He reached into his pocket and found what he was looking for. As his closed hand found its way back out into view, he opened his fingers to reveal a piece from a jigsaw puzzle. It was the piece he had taken that day when he and his grandfather spent their day together at Mirror Lake, making the puzzle which was a picture of Mount Rainier. He looked at the piece, worn from all of the years he had carried it with him in his pocket. It was a powerful remembrance of his grandfather. The piece had served as a bit of a good luck charm for Billy over the years, but most of all, it had served as a reminder of the many positive lessons about people and life that his grandfather had taught him. The edges were now frayed and the actual picture was peeling from its backing, but the picture was still clear. It was the summit of Mount Rainier, exactly where Billy was standing at this moment in time.

He looked at the piece that lay in his hand and thought to himself how lucky he was to have experienced all that he had experienced in his life to this point. How lucky he was to have had his parents and to have grown up where he did. How lucky he was to have gone to college and graduate school, allowing him the opportunity to learn and to meet so many wonderful people who had become part of his own puzzle. He thought about his lovely wife at home and their three children and, although she was afraid for him to attempt this climb, how she had encouraged him out of love, knowing full well that it was something he needed to do for himself. He thought about how lucky he had been to experience his good health and about what he had just accomplished, climbing Mount Rainier. And then, he thought about his grandfather and the many wonderful memories he had of his visits to his grandfather's cottage at Mirror Lake. Billy thought about his grandfather and what a special person, what a special piece he had been in his life, his puzzle. He looked again at the piece from the puzzle, and then tilted his head back and looked to the sky above. Holding the piece from the puzzle in his hand, he stretched his arm toward the blue sky directly above him and then, quietly, with almost a certain reverence, said to the sky above, "Papa, I did it. This one was for you!"

Just then, a gust of wind came up and blew swirling snow into his face, forcing him to turn his head and squint his eyes. "Don't start now, dangit! I still have to get down you know," he said, talking to the spirit of the mountain as much as to himself. He took one last look. It was a magnificent view, and yet he thought to himself: As much of the world as I can see from here, there is so much more that I want to see in my lifetime, so much more that I want to do.

He put the piece from the puzzle back into his pocket, zipped up his parka and put his gloves back on. The air was thin, stinging his lungs with every breath and he knew it was time to head down. He grabbed his ice axe and surveyed the vista one final time. Ah, this indeed was a special place. As he took his first step to descend the mountain, the wind swirled around him one final time and the spray of snow on his cheeks had a familiar feel to it. It was as though he were right back at Mirror Lake on one of those cold, winter days.

He thought to himself, Oh, how I do love this view, this place, this life. Yes, this was a good place to be and this had been a very special day.

Maybe, just maybe, tomorrow would be even better...